W9-AAX-624

Bedtime Favorites

Disney PRESS

New York

TABLE OF CONTENTS

MONSTERS, INC.
The Spooky Sleepover 5

THE LION KING
Simba's Big Secret 23

BAMBI
The Secret Adventure 39

LILO & STITCH
Doggone It, Stitch 57

DONALD DUCK
Donald Duck Goes Camping 75

PINOCCHIO
A Nose for Trouble 89

BROTHER BEAR
A Magical Journey 107

CINDERELLA
Bedtime for Gus 125

RATATOUILLE
Remy Becomes a Chef 135

TOY STORY & BEYOND
The Shadow Game 149

FINDING NEMO
Nemo and the Surprise Party 159

DUMBO
A Brand-New Act 177

CHICKEN LITTLE
A Day to Remember 195

THE ARISTOCATS
The Coziest Carriage 213

SLEEPING BEAUTY
Aurora's Slumber Party 229

WINNIE THE POOH
Piglet's Night-Lights 239

MICKEY MOUSE
Mickey Mouse and the Pet Shop 257

CARS
Friday Night Fun 273

SNOW WHITE AND THE SEVEN DWARFS
Dream Tales 291

Collection Copyright © 2007 Disney Enterprises, Inc.

"The Spooky Sleepover" adapted from the story "The Spooky Slumber Party" written by Kim Ostrow and originally published in *Scary Storybook Collection* by Disney Press. Copyright © 2003 Disney Enterprises, Inc./Pixar. Based on the characters from the movie *Monsters, Inc.* Copyright © 2001 Disney Enterprises, Inc./Pixar.

"Simba's Big Secret" adapted from the book *Cave Secret* written by Ellen Weiss, illustrated by Robbin Cuddy, and originally published by Disney Press. Copyright © 2000 Disney Enterprises, Inc. Based on the characters from the movie *The Lion King.* Copyright © 1994 Disney Enterprises, Inc.

"The Secret Adventure" adapted by Annie Auerbach from the book *Three Best Friends* illustrated by Angel Rodriguez and Ivan Boix and originally published by Egmont. Copyright © 2006 Disney Enterprises, Inc. Based on the characters from the movie *Bambi.* Copyright © 1942 Disney Enterprises, Inc.

"Doggone It, Stitch" adapted from the story "Doggone It, Stitch" written by Barbara Bazaldua, illustrated by K. White Studios, and originally published in *Scholastic Yearbook 2004* by Scholastic Inc. Copyright © 2004 Disney Enterprises, Inc. Based on the characters from the movie *Lilo & Stitch.* Copyright © 2002 Disney Enterprises, Inc.

"Donald Duck Goes Camping" adapted by Satia Stevens from the book *Donald Duck Goes Camping* originally published by Western Publishing Company. Copyright © 1977 Disney Enterprises, Inc. Based on the characters from the movies *The Wise Little Hen* Copyright © 1934 Disney Enterprises, Inc. and *Donald's Nephews* Copyright © 1938 Disney Enterprises, Inc.

"A Nose for Trouble" adapted from the book *A Nose for Trouble* written by Ronald Kidd, illustrated by Peter Emslie and Niall Harding, and originally published by Advance Publishers. Copyright © 1998 Disney Enterprises, Inc. Based on the characters from the movie *Pinocchio.* Copyright © 1940 Disney Enterprises, Inc.

"A Magical Journey" adapted from the book *A Magical Journey* adapted by Erin Hall and originally published by Random House. Copyright © 2003 Disney Enterprises, Inc. Based on the movie *Brother Bear.* Copyright © 2003 Disney Enterprises, Inc.

"Bedtime for Gus" adapted from the story "Bedtime for Gus" written by Catherine Hapka, illustrated by Design Rights International, and originally published in *5-Minute Bedtime Stories* by Disney Press. Copyright © 2000 Disney Enterprises, Inc. Based on the characters from the movie *Cinderella.* Copyright © 1950 Disney Enterprises, Inc.

"Remy Becomes a Chef" based on the movie *Ratatouille.* Copyright © 2007 Disney Enterprises, Inc./Pixar.

"The Shadow Game" adapted from the book *Jessie* written by Liane Onish and originally published by Disney Mouse Works. Copyright © 1999 Disney Enterprises, Inc. Based on the characters from the movies *Toy Story* Copyright © 1995 Disney Enterprises, Inc. and *Toy Story 2* Copyright © 1999 Disney Enterprises, Inc./Pixar. Original *Toy Story* elements © Disney Enterprises, Inc.

"Nemo and the Surprise Party" written by Amy Edgar. Copyright © 2007 Disney Enterprises, Inc./Pixar. Based on the characters from the movie *Finding Nemo.* Copyright © 2003 Disney Enterprises, Inc./Pixar.

"A Brand-New Act" adapted from the book *Dumbo and His New Act,* originally published by Scholastic Inc. Copyright © 2003 Disney Enterprises, Inc. Based on the characters from the movie *Dumbo.* Copyright © 1941 Disney Enterprises, Inc.

"A Day to Remember" adapted from the book *Who's That Chicken?* adapted by Kirsten Larsen and originally published by Disney Press. Copyright © 2005 Disney Enterprises, Inc./Pixar. Based on the movie *Chicken Little.* Copyright © 2005 Disney Enterprises, Inc./Pixar.

"The Coziest Carriage" adapted by Lara Bergen from a story in the book *Un Mondo di Amicizia,* written by Augusto Macchetto and Paola Mulazzi; illustrated by Alan Batson, Mara Damiani, and Silvano Scolari; and originally published by Disney Libri. Copyright © 2003 Disney Enterprises, Inc. Based on the characters from the movie *The Aristocats.* Copyright © 1970 Disney Enterprises, Inc. *The Aristocats* is based on the book by Thomas Rowe.

"Aurora's Slumber Party" adapted from an original story in *The Princess Party Book* written by Mary Man-Kong, illustrated by Francesco Legramandi and Gabriella Matta, and originally published by Random House. Copyright © 2005 Disney Enterprises, Inc. Based on the characters from the movie *Sleeping Beauty.* Copyright © 1959 Disney Enterprises, Inc.

"Piglet's Night-Lights" adapted from the book *Piglet's Night Light.* Copyright © 2003 Disney Enterprises, Inc. *Winnie the Pooh* based on the "Winnie the Pooh" works by A.A. Milne and E.H. Shepard. All rights reserved.

"Mickey Mouse and the Pet Shop" adapted from the book *Mickey Mouse and the Pet Shop* written by Mary Packard, illustrated by Guell, and originally published by Golden Books Publishing Co. Copyright © 1997 Disney Enterprises, Inc. Based on the characters from the movies *Steamboat Willie* Copyright © 1928 Disney Enterprises, Inc. and *The Moose Hunt* Copyright © 1931 Disney Enterprises, Inc.

"Friday Night Fun" written by Amy Edgar. Copyright © 2007 Disney Enterprises, Inc./Pixar. Based on the characters from the movie *Cars.* Copyright © 2006 Disney Enterprises, Inc./Pixar. Disney/Pixar elements © Disney/Pixar; Hudson Hornet is a trademark of DaimlerChrysler Corporation; Fiat is a trademark of Fiat S.p.A.; Chevrolet Impala is a trademark of General Motors; Porsche is a trademark of Porsche; Mercury is a registered trademark of Ford Motor Company; Cadillac Range background inspired by the Cadillac Ranch by Ant Farm (Lord, Michels and Marquez) © 1974.

"Dream Tales" adapted from the story "Bad Dreams" written by Catherine Hapka, illustrated by Design Rights International, and originally published in *5-Minute Bedtime Stories* by Disney Press. Copyright © 2000 Disney Enterprises, Inc. Based on the characters from the movie *Snow White and the Seven Dwarfs.* Copyright © 1937 Disney Enterprises, Inc.

Unless otherwise noted, all illustrations are by the Disney Storybook Artists.

All rights reserved. Published by Disney Press, an imprint of Disney Book Group. No part of this book may be reproduced or transmitted in any form or by any means, electronic or mechanical, including photocopying, recording, or by any information storage and retrieval system, without written permission from the publisher.

For information address Disney Press, 114 Fifth Avenue, New York, New York 10011-5690.

Printed in the United States of America

First Edition

10 9 8 7 6 5 4 3 2 1

G942-9090-6   11248

This book is set in 18-point Goudy Infant.

ISBN-13: 978-1-4231-5817-2

ISBN-10: 1-4231-5817-2

Visit www.disneybooks.com

SUSTAINABLE FORESTRY INITIATIVE

Certified Chain of Custody
40% Certified Forests,
60% Certified Fiber Sourcing

www.sfiprogram.org

PWC-SFICOC-260

DISNEY·PIXAR
MONSTERS, INC.

The Spooky Sleepover

It was a quiet morning at Monsters, Inc. James P. Sullivan, also known as Sulley, had gotten in early to catch up on his paperwork. He smiled as he reviewed the monthly laugh reports.

At Monsters, Inc., it was the monsters' job to go to the human world and made kids laugh. The laughs were used as energy for the city of Monstropolis. It had been Sulley's idea, and now he was president of Monsters, Inc. He was glad everything was going so well.

Suddenly, the phone rang. "Hello?" said Sulley.

"It's dispatch," said the voice on the other end of the line. "Annual slumber party at little Shannon Brown's house. Waxford is out sick. We need a replacement."

"I'll get right on it," replied Sulley. He knew that there would be a lot of kids at the party, and he wanted to make sure he had a monster there to tell jokes and capture laughs.

Sulley thought hard about who to send. He wanted to put his best monster on the case. He smiled to himself. Who better for the job than his one-eyed pal, Mike Wazowski? Mike was Monsters, Inc.'s top laugh collector. He could make anyone laugh. Sulley knew his best friend would be perfect for the job.

Mike was in the locker room getting ready for work. He had just finished putting his contact lens—which was the size of a pizza—in his one eye when Sulley walked in. Sulley explained the situation to Mike.

"I'm your man," Mike said confidently.

"Great!" Sulley exclaimed. Whistling, he went back to his office to finish his laugh reports.

"Piece of cake," Mike said as a door slid into his station on the Laugh Floor. "One joke and I'll collect enough energy for the year!" Then Mike opened the door and walked through the closet in Shannon

Brown's room. It was empty.

"Uh . . . hello?" Mike called. He looked around the room. He peeked under the bed—but there was no one there. Some party, he thought. I wonder where everyone is. Maybe I should go back. Just as Mike started walking toward the closet, he heard the sound of laughter.

"All right, now we are in business!" Mike exclaimed. "Kids, prepare to laugh."

Just then, thunder cracked across the sky, and a flash of lightning lit up the dark room. Mike jumped. If there was one thing he didn't like, it was a thunderstorm.

"I'm okay! I'm fine!" Mike shouted. Then he ran to the closet door to return to the factory.

Mike jiggled the doorknob, but it just opened into the closet, not the Laugh Floor at Monsters, Inc. There was no way out.

Mike soon realized that lightning must have struck the door and broken it. "Don't panic, don't panic," he told himself, his voice shaking. He knew he had to find the slumber party and another closet door—fast. Otherwise, who knew how long he'd be stuck there?

Mike took a deep breath and headed into the dark hallway. He was sure he heard laughter coming from somewhere. Now all he had to do was find it. As he started walking, the floor made a noise beneath him. *Crrreeaak!*

Halfway down the hallway, Mike stopped and looked around. There were some paintings on the wall that looked very creepy to him. They gave Mike goose bumps, and he was pretty sure the people in the paintings were staring right at him! "I gotta get out of here," Mike muttered to himself as he continued down the hallway. Then he saw something and froze.

Mike couldn't believe his eye. Sitting at the end of the hall was a large furry creature with fangs. It was panting heavily.

"Oh, man!" he cried. "Am I ever glad to see a fellow monster around here."

Taking a deep breath, Mike started to walk closer to the creature. Just as he did, the creature lunged toward him, knocking him down. Within seconds it began to lick Mike.

"Ahhhhhhhhhhh!" he screamed. "Dog breath!" Mike hated dogs!

He pushed the dog off him and ran as fast as he could into a nearby room. He slammed the door shut. He was safe—for now!

Meanwhile, back at Monsters, Inc., Sulley was working on the Laugh Floor. The floor manager came running over. "Sulley! Sulley!" he shouted. "Mike still hasn't returned from the slumber party. He's never been gone this long!"

When Sulley went to check on the door, he discovered it had malfunctioned. It didn't open into a closet. That meant that Mike was stuck in Shannon Brown's house!

"Uh-oh," said Sulley. "We gotta get Mike out of there."

Sulley brought in a maintenance crew to figure out how to fix the door.

Together the monsters pulled all the levers and pushed all the buttons on the door to try and get it to open properly.

When that didn't work, Sulley read
the emergency manuals. He and the
other monsters tried everything they
could. After a few hours, the door made a

clicking sound. It was working! Now it
would open into a different room at Shannon's house. The
monsters cheered.

Back in the house, Mike walked into the bathroom.

"Ouch!" the green monster squealed as he tripped on a yellow rubber ducky and went rolling across the floor. Finally, Mike crashed into the wall and stopped. Then he heard a lot of giggling down the hall.

Mike did not like this assignment—or this house—but he was determined to find the party. So he lifted himself off the floor and followed the laughter. But when he found the right door and opened it, it was quiet.

Slowly, Mike entered the dark, silent room. All of a sudden, a light went on! Mike jumped. Shannon Brown and all her friends started roaring with laughter! They thought Mike looked funny sneaking into the room.

"*Ahhhhhhhhh!*" Mike was so frightened that he couldn't stop yelling.

At that exact moment, the closet door opened and Sulley burst into the room. Sulley was so surprised to find Mike screaming that all he could do was let out an equally big scream. "*Ahhhhhhh!*" he yelled. Then he and Mike jumped toward each other and huddled in fright.

The girls at the slumber party laughed and laughed and laughed. A big blue monster with purple spots hugging a one-eyed little green monster was one of the funniest things they had ever seen.

Mike and Sulley looked at each other and smiled. Then Mike jumped to the floor, and they both took a bow. The kids cheered.

"Looks as if our work here is done," Sulley said. He and Mike headed through the closet door and back to the Monsters, Inc., Laugh Floor. They had filled so many canisters with laughs that Mike was named the top laugh collector that day.

"I was never scared for a second," said Mike, hoping Sulley would believe him.

"Me neither, buddy," Sulley replied, his big furry fingers crossed behind his back. "Me neither."

Simba's Big Secret

Simba and Nala were best friends. The lion cubs did everything together. They splashed in the water hole, snuck up on bugs, and raced through the high grass. They liked to tell each other secrets, too.

"I'm a little scared of mice," Nala told Simba one day. "Don't tell anybody."

"Don't worry, I won't," Simba said. "I get scared of the dark sometimes."

"Your secret is safe with me," said Nala.

Simba smiled at her. "Thanks," he said. "You're a good friend."

One day, Simba and his father, Mufasa, were out for a walk.

"Look at that little mouse stuffing her cheeks with seeds," said Mufasa.

"That's so funny!" said Simba. "I don't know why Nala's scared of mice."

"I remember when I was a cub. I was scared of mice, too!" Mufasa said with a chuckle.

Nala was just on the other side of the hill, chasing butterflies. She heard Simba talking with his dad, and she got really mad.

Later, Nala went to find Simba.

"You promised not to tell my secret!" she told him angrily. "And now your father knows. He'll tell everybody, and they'll all laugh at me! That's the last time I'm going to trust you."

"I'm sorry, Nala! Please don't stop trusting me!" Simba

pleaded. "I'll never tell anyone else what you say, I promise."

"Well . . ." said Nala, "we'll see."

Nala didn't stop playing with Simba, but she did stop telling him secrets.

A few weeks later, Nala finally changed her mind.

"I'm going to tell you a secret," she said to Simba, "but it's a really big one. If you tell this time, I'll be so mad at you I won't be your friend anymore."

"I promise I won't say anything!" said Simba.

"Okay," said Nala. "Here's the secret: I found a huge cave yesterday, down in the red cliffs. But I was with my mother, so I couldn't go in. I'm going back to explore it today."

"Can I come with you?" Simba asked.

"No, I want to go by myself," she replied as she walked away. "Maybe you can come some other day."

Simba played all day without Nala. A little before dinner, he began to wonder when she was coming back.

Nala's mother was wondering where her daughter was, too. "Simba," she asked, "do you have any idea where Nala is? Did she mention anything to you about going somewhere new or different?"

"No," he answered. He could not look her in the eye. It was the first time he had not told a grown-up the truth. But he'd made a promise to Nala, and he didn't want to break it.

The sun went down and the moon shone in the sky. Now Simba was starting to worry about Nala.

Nala's mother paced back and forth. "Where could she be?" she kept asking.

Simba wished he could tell her.

A couple of hours later, Nala still hadn't returned. The whole pride was worried about her.

Sarabi, Simba's mother, went to her son. "Do you know where Nala is?" she asked.

"I can't tell," said Simba. "It's a secret."

"A secret? What kind of a secret?" his mother asked.

"A big secret. I can't tell, no matter what!" he cried, explaining how mad Nala had been when he'd told Mufasa she was afraid of mice.

"Simba," said his mother, "you're a good friend to try not to tell Nala's secret. But there are some secrets that are good to keep and others that are important to tell."

"How do you know the difference?" asked Simba.

"If you think about it," Sarabi replied, "you will know in your heart if something is a good secret or a bad secret. Nala could be in trouble."

Simba thought about what his mother had said. He decided that he had to tell everyone where Nala was.

He pointed across the Pride Lands to the red cliffs. "She's over there," Simba said, "in a cave."

Sarabi hugged her son. "That was the right thing to do. Now, let's go find Nala."

The whole pride hurried across the grasslands to the red cliffs.

"Nala!" called her mother.

"*Naaalaa!*" Simba yelled.

There was only silence, and the cry of the hyenas.

"Nala!" her mother called again.

Then, at last, they heard a small voice. "M-mother?" It was Nala!

The lions rushed to where the voice had come from. It was the entrance to a cave, but it was almost completely blocked. A rock slide had trapped the little cub!

The lions dug and dug, and finally they had cleared the rocks away.

Nala rushed out of the cave and ran to her mother.

"Nala! I was so worried about you!" her mother cried.

"I'm sorry!" said Nala. "I was so scared! I'll never go anywhere without telling you again!"

A few minutes later, Simba walked over to his friend and hung his head. "I'm sorry I told your secret, Nala," he said. "Please don't be too mad at me."

"Why would I be mad at you?" said Nala. "If you hadn't said anything, I'd still be here. It was a stupid secret, and I'm really glad you told it!"

When they got home, it was time for bed. Nala and Simba snuggled together. "I'm so happy to be back!" she exclaimed.

"I'm happy you're home, too," said Simba. "And that's not a secret!"

Nala smiled, and they drifted off to sleep, dreaming of their next adventure together.

The Secret Adventure

Early one morning, Thumper the bunny hopped over to a thicket. "Bambi! Bambi! Wake up!" he whispered to the sleeping fawn.

Bambi stirred and gave a great big yawn. "Mmmm, I'll be right there," he mumbled. Sleepily, he stood up, trembling a little in the morning chill. Thumper hopped off and motioned for Bambi to follow him.

"I have to tell my mother where we're going," Bambi said.

Thumper stopped and gave Bambi a serious look. "You can't do that," he said. "It's a secret. Besides, she'd never let us go."

The friends hopped off to find Flower.

A few minutes later, Bambi and Thumper spotted their skunk friend. "Good morning, Flower," they said.

"Thumper wants to go on a secret adventure," Bambi said. "Do you want to come along?"

"Oh, gosh! I do," Flower said shyly. "But would you tell me what we're doing?"

Bambi looked at Thumper eagerly. He wanted to know, too.

Thumper puffed up his chest and said proudly, "I want to show you what the beavers build on water!"

Bambi and Flower looked at each other. They didn't understand how anyone could build something on water. But it sure sounded exciting.

The three friends didn't notice a red bird perched on a branch above them.

The youngsters are heading out on an adventure all by themselves, the bird said to himself. I wonder if their mothers know. I'd better fly over and tell them.

"Maybe it would be good for them to explore the forest on their own," Bambi's mother said to the bird, whose name was Red. "After all, there are three of them. Do you mind keeping an eye on them? Let me know if they go near the waterfall. Bambi hasn't tried swimming yet."

Red agreed and then flew off to tell Thumper's mother.

Meanwhile, Thumper and Flower were hard at work, trying to push Bambi through a tight thicket. He was stuck!

"Why are we going this way?" Bambi asked. "Why can't we go the regular way?"

"Shhh!" Thumper whispered. "We have to go this way. We are really close to the meadow where all the bunnies graze—including my mama," he explained quietly. "If she sees us, we won't be able to go on our secret adventure. She'll say I have to stay and look after my silly sisters!"

Suddenly some branches gave way and the three friends fell out onto the meadow.

Bambi, Thumper, and Flower quickly ran back into the
bushes. They peeked out to see if the bunnies had spotted them.

"No one is looking at us," Thumper said. "My mama is
talking with her friend Red. I think we're safe. Come on,
let's go!"

But they had been spotted! Thumper's sisters had seen everything. They wanted to know what their big brother was up to, so they followed him. So did Red.

The three friends continued walking through the woods. Soon they came to a stream. Thumper looked around. He was not sure where to go next.

Suddenly a beaver with big teeth and a large, flat tail walked up to them. "Who are you?" Bambi asked.

"My name is Slap," the beaver said. "Where are you going?"

Thumper hopped forward. "I wanted to show my friends what the beavers build on the river," he explained.

"We call it a dam," said Slap, "and I can show you the way."

A little while later, they arrived at the dam.

"Here we are," Slap said proudly. Everywhere along the river, the beavers were busy. Some were in the water pushing logs, while others were chopping down the trees along the riverbank with their strong teeth.

"Come out onto the dam," Slap offered.

Carefully the three friends stepped out onto the logs. Thumper and Flower went first and Bambi followed, a bit unstable on his legs. Soon they were balancing on the logs among the working beavers.

"Hey, this is fun!" Thumper shouted, thumping his foot in excitement.

"Why do they call you Slap?" Flower asked their new beaver friend shyly.

"I'll show you," Slap replied. He started slapping the logs with his flat tail. "I'm the best slapper in the whole river!" he exclaimed.

The entire dam shook so much when Slap was slapping that a log broke loose and started drifting downriver.

"Help! Help, Thumper!" four little voices suddenly cried.

It was Thumper's four younger sisters! They had gone out on the dam just as Slap had slapped the logs. Now the log they were sitting on was floating away!

"Oh, no! My sisters!" Thumper exclaimed. "We have to rescue them!"

"Hurry—they are headed toward the waterfall!" Slap shouted.

All the beavers jumped into the water and quickly swam toward the log. High above, Red saw the whole thing and swiftly flew off to tell Mama Bunny and Bambi's mother.

Thumper's sisters held on to each other and tried to balance so they would not fall into the river. But they were getting close to the waterfall!

A few minutes later, Slap and the two other beavers reached the runaway log. They slapped their tails with all their might, and slowly but surely, they got the log to the riverbank. Bambi stood in the water with Thumper perched on his head. One by one, Thumper pulled his sisters to safety.

Once everyone was back on land, Thumper thanked the beavers for their bravery.

"You're welcome," said Slap. "Can you find your way home from here?"

"Nothing to it," Thumper said confidently. "We live just around that thicket, and to the right."

Thumper began to lead the others through the woods. But he couldn't seem to find the path home, so they kept walking and walking.

After a while, it began to get dark in the forest. The trees blocked the light from the fading sun, and the branches swayed, casting scary shadows all around.

"Uh, Thumper," Bambi said, "I think we might be lost."

"Oh, don't be silly," Thumper said, looking back at them. "It's just like in the daytime . . . only darker. There's nothing to be afraid of here—especially when you're with the bravest rabbit in the forest!" he bragged.

Suddenly Thumper hopped into something. *"Aaaahhh!"* he screamed.

Luckily it was not a monster that Thumper had run into. It was his own mother! For his mother, as well as Bambi's, had finally found them.

"Oh, I'm so glad you are safe!" cried Bambi's mother as she led them into the meadow, where there was more sunlight. "Red was keeping an eye on you. He told us what happened."

Until now the friends had not noticed the bird, who was flitting in the air above them.

Thumper's mother tapped her foot angrily. "Thumper! What does your father always tell you?"

Thumper looked down at the ground. He didn't like to be scolded. "Never go off on your own without telling someone first," he replied.

"That's right," Thumper's mother said. "You all must promise never to do that again."

54

They all agreed, though Thumper didn't seem too happy about it.

"Good," said Bambi's mother. "Now let's go home. The sun has started to set."

Soon the group returned home.

"Good night, everyone," Flower said.

"Good night, Flower!" the others called.

"Good night, Bambi," Thumper said.

"Good night, Thumper," Bambi replied. Then he whispered, "Thanks for taking me on a secret adventure."

Thumper smiled. He and his family went to their burrow. Soon Thumper was fast asleep, dreaming of his next adventure.

Not far away, Bambi's eyelids fluttered shut. It had been a long and exciting day, and he was tired.

Moonlight beamed over the meadow and everything in the forest was still and peaceful . . . at last.

Doggone It, Stitch!

Stitch, an alien who lived on Earth, was sitting in the living room waiting for his friend, Lilo, to come home from school. Just then, Lilo burst into the house carrying a puppy.

"Hi, Stitch!" Lilo said excitedly. "My neighbor Leilani asked me to take care of her puppy, Rover, while she visits her grandmother."

"Stitch wants to listen to music," Stitch said.

"Not now," Lilo answered. "I have to take care of Rover."

Stitch watched Lilo make a bed for Rover. He watched her scratch his ears and rub his tummy. Stitch was bored. He wanted Lilo to play with him.

"Can we listen to music *now?*" Stitch asked.

"I want to teach Rover some new tricks," Lilo said. She showed the puppy how to roll over. Then she threw him a ball and gave him treats.

Lilo taught Rover tricks all afternoon while Stitch watched quietly. The dog learned to sit, to beg, and to stay.

"Way to go, Rover!" Lilo said, encouragingly. "You're a good doggie!" She patted him on the head.

"Music, now?" Stitch asked again.

"Later," Lilo replied. "Rover's hungry."

That evening, Nani, Lilo's older sister, came home from work. She and Lilo watched Rover play tug-of-war with the kitchen rug. "Oh, isn't he cute!" Nani exclaimed. They laughed at everything Rover did. They didn't pay any attention to poor Stitch.

Stitch went upstairs. He felt a little sad. Maybe if I act like a puppy, he thought, Lilo will play with me. He flopped on the bed and went to sleep.

The next morning, Stitch tried to act like Rover. He hid Lilo's shoes and chewed the kitchen rug. But that only made Lilo angry.

"You need a time-out," she told Stitch. "Go to our room while I take Rover for a walk."

Stitch waited until Lilo and Rover were gone. Then he hurried outside and ran toward town.

When Lilo and Rover came home, it was time for Lilo to go to her hula class. Lilo couldn't find Stitch anywhere. She wondered why he wasn't home. Stitch loved dancing the hula.

I guess I'll have to go without him, Lilo thought.

Stitch still wasn't home when Lilo returned. Lilo asked Nani and her friend, David, if they had seen him.

Before they could answer, Cobra Bubbles called. He was a social worker that Lilo and Nani knew.

"You need to hide Stitch," Cobra told Lilo. "Two scientists from the Center for the Study of Aliens are looking for him. They want to take him to their laboratory."

"But I don't know where Stitch is!" Lilo exclaimed. "He's gone!"

"Well, I suggest you find him before the scientists do," Cobra replied.

Lilo and Nani hurried to town to look for Stitch. David drove to the beach to search.

"Stitch has been acting weird all day," Lilo told Nani. "His badness level was way up. He hid my shoes and chewed the rug. He acted just like Rover!"

Suddenly, Lilo knew where Stitch had gone. "Stitch probably thought I liked Rover better because he was a puppy. I bet Stitch went to the animal shelter to watch the puppies!" She grabbed Nani's hand and pulled her toward the shelter.

When Lilo and Nani arrived, Stitch was there.

"Stitch learning to be cute like puppy," he explained when he saw them. "So Lilo like him again."

"Stitch, I like you just the way you are," Lilo answered. "Now, let's go home!"

But when they started to leave, they saw the two scientists coming toward them. "Nani!" Lilo cried. "We've got to do something!"

Nani spotted two dust mops in the shelter closet. She tied the mops on to Stitch so he looked like a long-haired puppy.

Lilo put a leash on Stitch, and they walked slowly out of the shelter and past the scientists. The scientists watched Stitch suspiciously.

Just then, Cobra Bubbles and David drove up.

"Hey, scientists!" David called. "We just saw an alien heading out to sea. You'd better hurry if you want to catch it. Hop in, and we'll take you there." The scientists jumped into the car, and Cobra Bubbles and David sped off.

Stitch was safe!

Lilo, Nani, and Stitch went home, where Rover was waiting patiently. Stitch went over to the dog and pointed to his paw. "Stitch show you how to shake your paw," the alien said.

Lilo smiled. She was happy Stitch wanted to make friends with Rover, but now it was time for the puppy to go home.

A few minutes later, David and Cobra came in. "The scientists are heading out to sea to look for Stitch," Cobra said. "He's safe for now."

"And look what I found at the beach," David said. He lifted a kitten out of a bag and set her on the floor.

"I thought she needed a good home," he said.

The kitten began to explore the room. After a few minutes, David left to go to work.

"How cute," Lilo said. Stitch watched everyone play with the kitten. Then the kitten spotted the alien and ran to him. Stitch scooped her up and gave her a big hug. The kitten was soft and cuddly. She began to purr.

Stitch found some string and began to play with the kitten. She darted this way and that, trying to grab the string as Stitch moved it around.

Then the alien took the kitten outside. "Stitch teach you tricks now," he said. He taught the kitten to come when he called and to stay in one spot.

Lilo watched from the window. "Stitch is really good at having a pet," she said.

Nani glanced outside. "Yes, he seems happy," she remarked.

After a while, it was time to eat. "Dinner!" Lilo called.

Instead of racing to the table as he usually did, Stitch got some food and fed the kitten first. Then he sat down and ate with Lilo and Nani.

After dinner, Stitch began to play with the kitten some more. But the kitten had had a long day. She climbed into Stitch's lap and fell asleep.

Lilo and Nani went into the kitchen and began frosting a cake that Nani had made earlier.

A few minutes later, Stitch made a bed for the kitten. Then he went into the kitchen. "Can Stitch keep the kitten?" he asked.

"I think the kitten has already adopted you," Nani replied. "You're her family now." She pointed to the cake.

"The frosting reads '*Ohana*, Stitch," Lilo said. "And you know what that means."

Stitch nodded. "'*Ohana* means family—and that means nobody gets left behind."

Nani smiled. "Now let's eat some cake and go to bed. Tomorrow we have to show the kitten her new neighborhood."

Donald Duck Goes Camping

"Yippee!" Huey, Dewey, and Louie cried. They had just found out that their uncle, Donald Duck, was taking them camping.

Donald and his nephews began to load their gear into the car.

"I've got the tent and the food," Donald said.

"Here are the fishing poles," Huey said.

"Don't forget the sleeping bags," Louie reminded them.

"I'm bringing a camping guidebook," said Dewey. "There's all kinds of great information in here about wildlife. You never know— we might need it."

"You don't need a guidebook," Donald said confidently.
"I know everything there is to know about camping."

Donald and his nephews hopped into the car and headed
toward the forest. A couple of hours later, they arrived in the
woods and found a camping spot.

Huey and Louie helped their uncle put up the tent while
Dewey read from the
guidebook.

When they were finished setting up the tent, they put their food inside a wooden locker to keep it away from wild animals.

"The guidebook says to hang the food locker from a tree," said Dewey. "It says bears will eat almost *anything*!"

"I already told you, I know everything there is to know about camping," Donald said. "Animals aren't going to take food from me!"

Just then, two squirrels scampered down from a big oak tree and snatched a bag of peanuts.

"Hey!" Donald shouted as the squirrels scurried back up the tree. "Come back here!"

"The guidebook says it's good to share with *little* animals," said Louie. "But we shouldn't try to share with bears!"

"I don't care what the book says. Those are *my* peanuts!" replied Donald. He grabbed an ax from the camping supplies.

With all his might, Donald swung the ax toward the base of the tree. *Crack!* He chopped a large hole in the tree trunk, and a stream of acorns spilled onto the ground.

"Why did you do that, Uncle Donald?" asked Dewey.

"You spilled the squirrels' supply of acorns for the winter."

"They stole my peanuts," said Donald, angrily.

The squirrels glared at Donald Duck and then darted away.

Donald chuckled. "What silly little animals!"

A little while later, Huey looked up from his camping book. "Uh-oh!" he said, pointing into the woods. A large bear was charging toward them!

"Run!" Donald shouted. He and his nephews scrambled up some nearby trees.

The bear thundered to a stop at the picnic table, and began to sniff at the food locker. The two squirrels had arrived with the bear, and they sat on a branch overlooking the campsite. With one swipe of his big paw, the bear broke open the food locker. Then he took a baked ham and ambled off.

"The guidebook was right," said Huey. "We should have hung the locker from a tree."

Donald climbed down to the ground. "I don't need a book to tell me what to do!" he said, annoyed.

The two squirrels ran along the tree branches and chattered at Donald again. This time, they seemed to be laughing at him.

"I'll get even with you!" Donald yelled. He climbed toward the squirrels. Just as he was about to grab them, they leaped onto a thin branch that was high above the river.

"I've got you now," said Donald. He crawled out onto the branch.

"Unca Donald!" Dewey shouted. "The book says to stay off small branches!"

Crrrrack! Suddenly, the branch broke, and Donald fell into the river.

The water swiftly carried him downstream. His nephews ran alongside him. Soon they heard the thundering sound of a waterfall.

"Help!" Donald cried. "Pull me out!" He tried to swim toward the riverbank, but the current was too strong.

Up in the trees, the squirrels chattered gleefully.

"Shame on you!" Louie scolded the squirrels. "How would you feel if your uncle was headed toward a waterfall?" The squirrels stopped laughing and darted into the underbrush.

In the river, Donald spotted a big rock and grabbed on to it. "Do something!" he called to his nephews. "Anything! Look in the guidebook!"

Huey, Dewey, and Louie started flipping through the camping guide, searching for a way to help their uncle. They only looked up when the squirrels returned—with a brown beaver!

The beaver waddled to a tree that stood beside the river and began to gnaw at it.

"What's he doing?" asked Louie.

"He's trying to help!" Dewey replied. "If the tree falls into the river, it might be long enough to reach Uncle Donald. Please hurry!"

A few minutes later, the tree fell over with a crash. It landed next to the rock that Donald was clinging to.

Donald crept along the tree trunk toward dry land. Soon he was safely ashore. Huey, Dewey, and Louie gave him a big hug.

"You made it!" Dewey exclaimed.

"Were you scared?" Louie asked.

"Don't worry, Uncle Donald," Huey said. "I would have thought of something."

Donald didn't answer. Instead, he ran toward his car.

"Where are you going?" his nephews called. "Aren't you going to thank the animals who rescued you?"

Donald just hopped in the car and sped away. Huey, Dewey, and Louie looked at each other and shrugged.

Donald returned in an hour. His car was filled with presents for the animals who had helped him. He had nuts for the squirrels, branches for the beaver, and a big bag of seeds for the birds.

The animals and birds were delighted and began to munch on their treats.

Donald also had a sack of cement and a trowel.

"What's that for?" Louie asked.

"You'll see," said Donald.

He mixed the cement into a thick paste, and spread it with the trowel over the hole in the squirrels' big oak tree.

Donald's nephews watched him patch the hole. "Do you really know how to fix trees?" asked Huey.

"I do now," Donald said sheepishly. "I read all about it in the camping guidebook. You can learn a lot from books, you know!"

Walt Disney's Pinocchio

A Nose for Trouble

School was out for the day, and Pinocchio was ready to have some fun. The puppet skipped down the cobblestone street, swinging his books.

A small figure followed him, clutching an umbrella. It was Pinocchio's pal, Jiminy Cricket. "Wait for me!" he called.

Jiminy caught up with Pinocchio in front of the small shop where the puppet lived with Geppetto, his father. Geppetto carved all sorts of things out of wood—but his greatest creation was Pinocchio. The night he'd finished carving Pinocchio, he'd wished the puppet were a real boy. Then the Blue Fairy appeared and brought Pinocchio to life. If the puppet proved himself worthy, someday he'd become a real boy.

Jiminy hopped onto Pinocchio's shoulder, and they went into the shop.

"Father, I'm home!" Pinocchio called. The only answer was the ticktock of a dozen clocks.

"Father?" Pinocchio asked. He went into the next room, and found Geppetto, seated at a workbench. The woodcarver looked up, surprised.

"Hello, son," he said. "I didn't hear you come in. You know how it is when you're working."

"What are you making?" Pinocchio asked.

"A cuckoo clock," Geppetto replied. "I even brought home a live bird for a model. That way I can carve the cuckoo just right." He pointed to a birdcage.

"May I take the bird out and play with him?" Pinocchio asked excitedly.

"I'm afraid not," said Geppetto. "You aren't the only one who's been watching him."

Geppetto nodded toward Figaro the cat, who was following the cuckoo's every move.

"Please?" begged Pinocchio. "I'll be careful."

"I'm sorry, son," Geppetto said gently. "I wouldn't want Figaro to chase him."

Pinocchio spent the afternoon in the workshop. Every few minutes he glanced up at the birdcage and imagined what fun it would be to have the cuckoo perch on his finger. Pinocchio had never held a live bird before, and he was very curious to find out if it would sing to him. Would it sit on his shoulder and go wherever he went? he wondered.

At the end of the day, Geppetto went out to the market. As soon as he left, Pinocchio hurried over to the birdcage.

"Pinocchio?" Jiminy said. "What are you doing?"

"Taking the bird out so we can visit," the puppet replied. "Don't worry."

As Pinocchio opened the cage door, Figaro jumped onto the table.

"Watch out!" Jiminy cried as the cat leaped toward the open birdcage.

Figaro was fast, but the cuckoo was faster. The bird zipped out of the cage.

Crash! Figaro hit the side of the cage.

The cuckoo flew around the room. "See?" Pinocchio told Jiminy. "I told you it would be fine."

"I don't know," the cricket murmured. "You shouldn't have disobeyed your father." The cuckoo darted in and out of the rafters, then began to investigate Geppetto's clocks. Wherever the bird went, Figaro followed him.

Jiminy climbed onto the windowsill to get a better view. All of a sudden, the cuckoo turned and began flying straight toward him!

"Look out!" cried Pinocchio.

Jiminy leaped to one side.

The cuckoo had just spotted an open window. With a happy cry, he flew past Jiminy and out of the shop.

Just then, Geppetto walked in. He glanced at the empty birdcage. "Pinocchio!" he yelled. "I told you not to open the cage! Now look what has happened! I'm very disappointed."

Panicked, Pinocchio looked around the room and spotted Figaro. "I didn't do it," he lied. "It was Figaro! He opened the birdcage and ate the cuckoo!"

"Figaro!" cried Geppetto.

He picked up the cat to scold him, which was lucky for Pinocchio, because at that moment the puppet's nose began to grow. It inched out farther and farther, until it was the length of a crayon. It was growing because he had lied. Pinocchio didn't want his father to realize he had told a lie. So he tried to hide his nose.

"Father," Pinocchio said, "I think I'll go to bed early tonight. I'm not feeling well."

By the time Pinocchio had gotten under the covers, his nose had grown another inch.

The next morning, Pinocchio got up before his father. He sneaked out of bed and ate a hasty breakfast. Then, throwing on his clothes, he headed for the door, calling, "Good-bye, Father! I'm off to school!"

Jiminy hurried along after him. He knew Pinocchio wasn't going to school, because his nose was growing again.

"Pinocchio," Jiminy said, "you must start telling the truth."

"I can't!" cried Pinocchio. "I'll get into too much trouble."

Pinocchio hurried through the village, asking people if they'd seen the cuckoo. Then he climbed the bell tower, and looked out across the sky. Next he bought a birdhouse and some seeds, hoping the cuckoo would stop by for a snack. But he didn't have any luck.

Wherever Pinocchio went, Jiminy Cricket followed along, trying to convince him to tell the truth. But Pinocchio wouldn't listen.

Pinocchio told lie after lie—about why he wasn't at school, where he was going, and what he was doing. Each time, his nose grew a little longer.

At the end of the day, Pinocchio's nose was longer than ever before—and he still hadn't found the cuckoo.

"Maybe you're right," Pinocchio said with a sigh. "It's time to tell the truth."

The puppet began to walk back through the streets of the village. Jiminy had to run ahead to clear a path. At last they got home, with Pinocchio arriving several seconds after Jiminy and his nose.

"Figaro didn't really eat the cuckoo," Pinocchio told his father. "I opened the birdcage, and the cuckoo flew away. I'm sorry I disobeyed you, but most of all, I'm sorry I lied."

As Pinocchio spoke, his nose became shorter and shorter, until it was back to its normal size.

"I'm glad you finally told the truth," said Geppetto. "And now I have something to show you."

He led Pinocchio inside, where something sat on the table, covered with a sheet. Had his father finished carving the clock? Geppetto drew aside the sheet, and under it was a birdcage— with the cuckoo inside!

"Where did you find him?" Pinocchio asked.

"He found me!" Geppetto exclaimed. "I was working on the clock today, and he flew in through the window. I think he likes it here!"

"He should," Pinocchio said. "It's the best home anyone could ever want."

After dinner, the cuckoo began to chirp. Geppetto played his concertina while Pinocchio and Figaro danced.

Before long, night had fallen. Pinocchio yawned. "I think it's time for bed," Geppetto said with a smile.

Pinocchio gave his father a hug and got into bed. The cuckoo sang sweetly, and everyone drifted off to sleep.

A Magical Journey

Once there was a boy named Kenai. When his oldest brother, Sitka, was lost in a bear-hunting accident, Kenai began to hate bears. Soon it was all he could think about.

Kenai did not know it, but Sitka had joined the Great Spirits in the sky. As an eagle spirit, Sitka watched over Kenai. Sitka saw that Kenai had become very angry. To teach him to love again, Sitka came down from the sky and magically changed Kenai into the thing he hated most—a bear!

Kenai felt different, but he didn't know why. He didn't realize he had been changed into a bear! Suddenly, a bolt of lightning hit the ground near him. He tumbled over a ledge and into a river far below.

When Kenai reached the shore, he looked into the water and saw a bear staring back at him! Horrified, he realized it was his reflection. He had to figure out how to turn himself back into a boy. He decided to find the mountain where the magical lights in the sky touched the earth. He thought he would be able to talk to his brother's spirit there.

Kenai set out on his journey and soon met two moose named Rutt and Tuke. He thought they might know where the mountain was. But the two silly moose were afraid of bears. They tried to hide and pretended Kenai hadn't seen them. "Uh, we're not here," they said.

When Kenai realized why they were hiding, he became upset.

"I'm not a bear!" he shouted. "I hate bears!"

"Well, gee," said Rutt, "you're one big beaver, eh."

"I'm not a beaver!" cried Kenai. "I'm a man!" But the moose didn't understand.

Kenai walked off. He didn't get very far when his foot got caught in a trap! As he dangled upside down, a bear cub approached.

"Hold still," the cub said. He swung a stick at Kenai, trying to help him down.

"Stop that!" cried Kenai. "I don't need some silly bear's help."

Kenai struggled for hours, but couldn't free himself. He realized he did need the cub's help. The cub told Kenai his name was Koda. He agreed to free Kenai if the bear promised to go with him to the Salmon Run. Kenai was desperate to get down, and he reluctantly agreed.

The two bears began their journey together. Kenai decided that he was going to break his word and leave Koda. But when Koda told him that the mountain where the lights touched the earth was close to the Salmon Run, Kenai figured he would travel with the cub after all.

Koda began to talk. Kenai was still annoyed that the cub had come with him, so he didn't say much. But Koda just kept talking and talking and talking.

Finally, Kenai was sick of it. "How about no talking?" he suggested.

"Okay!" Koda said cheerfully. "Then I'll sing!"

Kenai began to wonder how much longer he could stand being around the cub.

But as the days passed, Koda helped Kenai learn to act like a bear. And even though he still wanted to become human again, Kenai began to change his mind about Koda.

The two bears laughed and joked. They had become friends.

One day Rutt and Tuke ran into Kenai and Koda. They were scared because a hunter was following them.

Kenai remembered following tracks when he had gone hunting. "I've got an idea," he said.

Once, Kenai had ridden on a mammoth's back for fun. He realized that if he and his animal friends rode on some mammoths, the hunter would not be able to follow their tracks.

"Whoa! You've done this before?" Koda exclaimed as he followed Kenai onto a mammoth's tusks. Now *he* was learning from Kenai.

That night, Koda looked up at the lights in the sky. "My grandma's up there. And my granddad," he said. "Mom says the spirits make all the magical changes in the world."

"My brother's a spirit," said Kenai. "If it weren't for him, I wouldn't be here."

"Thanks!" Koda yelled to the sky. "If it weren't for you, I would've never met Kenai. I always wanted a brother."

The next morning
the two bears woke up
and looked around.

"So where are we?"
Kenai asked. But Koda
didn't know. They
were lost.

The bears jumped
off the mammoths
to try to figure out
which way to go.
The moose couldn't
get down and decided
to keep traveling with
the mammoths.

Kenai was very angry. He thought Koda had known the way.

"I'm sorry we're lost, okay?" said Koda. "I'll just go on my own, then." He walked away.

But Kenai had grown to care for Koda. He raced after his friend and found him near a cave.

On the cave walls, they saw a drawing of a hunter carrying a spear. The hunter was fighting a bear.

"Those monsters are really scary," Koda said, "especially with those sticks."

Kenai realized the cub was talking about hunters—not bears!

Finally, after a long journey, Kenai and Koda reached their destination. At first, Kenai was scared. He met all sorts of bears who seemed big and frightening.

As Kenai got to know the bears, he began to change his mind. They were friendly and told stories. They worked together and played together, just like people. Kenai was beginning to understand bears . . . and to like them. He and Koda jumped into the water and fished together, just like brothers.

When Kenai finally climbed the mountain where the lights in the sky touched the earth, his other brother, Denahi, had caught up with him. He was the hunter Kenai, Koda, and the moose had been running from.

As Kenai and Denahi fought, Sitka appeared and transformed Kenai back into a boy. But Kenai realized that Koda needed him. So he decided that he would stay a bear. Denahi understood, and he and the rest of the tribe came to love Kenai and Koda—two bears who became brothers.

Walt Disney's Cinderella

Bedtime for Gus

Cinderella looked out her bedroom window as the sun was setting over the horizon. The sky was golden and orange. In the distance, the clock in the tower of the castle read eight o'clock.

Cinderella leaned over and tapped gently on the walls of her attic room. "Bedtime, everyone!" she called.

Jaq, Suzy, Gus, and the other mice hurried out of their mouse hole. Cinderella did all of the household chores in her wicked stepmother's house. She never had time for fun, so the birds and mice were her only friends.

"Bedtime already?" Jaq cried.

"Buh-bedtime?" Gus asked. Gus was Cinderella's newest mouse friend. She had just rescued him from a trap that morning.

"Bedtime, Gus-Gus," Suzy explained. "Close eyes and . . . *zzzz* . . . fall asleep!"

Gus looked confused. He closed his eyes and started to tip over.

Jaq caught him. "Not *fall*, Gus-Gus," he said. "Fall asleep. Like this." He put his head on his hands and pretended to snore.

Cinderella laughed. "Falling asleep isn't all there is to bedtime," she said. "Gus has never lived in a house before. We'll have to teach him about getting ready for bed."

"Okay! Okay!" the other mice cried. "Show Gus-Gus!"

"First," Cinderella said, "you have to put on your pajamas."

She went to her dresser and pulled out a tiny pair of striped pajamas for Gus. "Here, try these on."

Soon all the mice were dressed in their pajamas. Gus even wore a pair of cozy slippers.

"That's better," Cinderella declared. "Pajamas are much more comfortable for sleeping than regular clothes."

Gus nodded. "Gus-Gus *loves* pajamas!" he exclaimed. "Gus-Gus wear pajamas all the time!"

Cinderella smiled. "I'm glad you like your pajamas Gus, but they are only for while you're sleeping."

The mouse nodded.

"Now sleep, Cinderella?" another mouse cried.

Cinderella smiled. "Not quite yet," she said to the young mouse. "First, wash your faces and brush your teeth. When you're all scrubbed and brushed, I'll kiss you good night, and then Suzy will tuck everyone in."

Gus began to brush his teeth. "Mmm-mmm," he said with a smile, tasting the minty toothpaste.

The other mice giggled and finished up. Gus watched carefully, and before long, he was done, too.

"Tuh-tuck in?" Gus asked.

Jaq pulled him toward the washbasin. "Not yet, Gus-Gus," he said. He handed him some soap.

Gus looked puzzled. But he watched as the other mice washed their faces with tiny cloths and patted themselves dry with some old rags. Then he did the same.

When the mice were all neat and clean, Cinderella kissed each of them good night. "It's time for everyone to go to sleep," she said sweetly.

"Follow me," Jaq told Gus. He ran over to his little bed and hopped in. The he pointed to the bed next to him. "That's your bed," he said. Gus grinned and got under the covers.

Suzy tucked in each of the mice.

"Story, Cinderella!" the mice cried. "Story!"

Cinderella smiled. "All right," she said. "Once upon a time, there was a young prince who lived in a beautiful castle. He had everything that money could buy—fine clothes, jewels, paintings, and more. But something was missing. He didn't have anyone special to love. . . ."

She continued the story for a long time. Each time she tried to stop, the mice begged for more. After a while, they couldn't keep their eyes open anymore. It was just too late.

132

When the last mouse had fallen asleep, Cinderella tiptoed to her own bed and climbed in, still thinking about the bedtime story. Dreaming up tales of adventure and romance made her forget her life of chores.

Gus began to snore. Cinderella giggled and pulled up her covers. She glanced once more at the clock on the castle tower. "Oh, my," she murmured sleepily. "If the mice had their way, I'd be telling tales until midnight!"

She snuggled against her pillow and yawned. "If only," she added sleepily, "some of my stories would come true. . . ."

The birds began to sing a lullaby, and soon Cinderella was fast asleep, dreaming that someday she'd live in a beautiful castle.

REMY BECOMES A CHEF

Deep in the French countryside lived a rat named Remy. He wasn't like the other rats—he hated eating garbage. He liked to eat fancy food like cheese and mushrooms instead.

Remy enjoyed sneaking into the kitchen of the cottage where the rats lived. There he would watch a chef named Gusteau on TV. Gusteau liked to say that anyone could cook. So Remy decided to learn how. He even read Gusteau's cookbook.

One day, Remy was in the kitchen looking for a spice for a dish he was making. The old woman who lived in the cottage had fallen asleep, but the TV was on. A reporter was saying that Gusteau had died. Remy was so shocked that he didn't realize the old woman had woken up.

The woman chased Remy around the room. She made such a mess that part of the ceiling came crashing down—along with the rats who lived in the attic!

The rats had to escape. They ran toward the river, but Remy stopped. He didn't want to leave without the cookbook. By the time Remy ran back for the book and got to the river, the other rats were already floating away. Remy didn't know if he could catch up. He threw the book into the water and hopped on top of it.

"Come on, son!" called Django, Remy's father. "You can make it!"

But the water moved too fast, and Remy got separated from his family. He went over a waterfall and when he landed, he found himself in a sewer. He was all alone, and he'd lost everything—except the cookbook. He pulled it out of the water and opened the pages to dry it out. All of a sudden, a picture of Gusteau seemed to come to life. "Go up and look around," he suggested. So Remy did.

Remy climbed through walls and pipes and eventually ended up on a rooftop. He realized he was in Paris—and only a couple of blocks away was Gusteau's restaurant!

Gusteau appeared again, and he and Remy peered down into the restaurant from a skylight. Remy was thrilled to see a real restaurant kitchen.

Then he saw a garbage boy named Linguini knock over a pot of soup. The boy added ingredients so that no one would notice, but he didn't know what he was doing.

"He's ruining the soup!" Remy cried. Just then the skylight window opened and he fell through—down into the kitchen!

Remy scrambled around, trying to escape. On the way to an open window, he passed the soup—it smelled disgusting!

"What are you waiting for?" Gusteau asked Remy. "You know how to fix it." Remy realized that Gusteau was right. He grabbed some spices, climbed up to the brim of the pot, and began to cook. When he turned around, the garbage boy was staring at him!

Remy began to run away, but the boy trapped him underneath a colander. Skinner, the head chef, had just appeared. "How dare you cook in my kitchen!" he thundered at the boy. While the chef yelled, a waiter took a bowl of the soup into the dining room. When he returned, he had good news: a critic had tasted the soup and loved it.

Remy was thrilled, but he had to get out of there! He moved toward the window, but the chef saw him. He ordered Linguini to get rid of the rat.

Linguini didn't have the heart to hurt Remy, though. Skinner had told Linguini that he'd be fired if he didn't make the soup again. Linguini knew he would lose his job. He told Remy all of this. Then he realized the rat understood him. "You can cook, right?" Linguini asked. Remy nodded.

Linguini asked Remy to help him. Remy realized Linguini needed him. Together, they came up with a system. Remy pulled Linguini's hair to tell him what to do.

At the restaurant, Remy hid under Linguini's chef hat so no one would find out about him. They were a great cooking team, and the customers loved everything Remy and Linguini made.

One night, outside the restaurant, Remy ran into his brother, Emile. Remy was thrilled. He hadn't thought he'd ever see his family again. Emile brought him to the sewer where their dad and the other rats had made their home. All of the rats were excited to see Remy and threw him a party.

As much as Remy loved his family and friends, he also loved being a chef. His father tried to explain that humans were dangerous and that they would always see him as a rat. But Remy thought he could change things. After all, he and Linguini were good friends. He decided to go back to the restaurant.

A couple of days later, Linguini found out that Gusteau was his father and had left the restaurant to him. Now Linguini was in charge!

Over the next few weeks, the restaurant became more and more popular. One night, some reporters showed up, and Linguini seemed more interested in speaking with them than cooking. He took credit for the dishes he and Remy had made. Remy was furious.

Then, a tough food critic named Ego showed up and challenged Linguini to cook for him.

When Remy and Linguini returned to the kitchen, Remy pulled Linguini's hair to show him how angry he was.

Linguini took Remy to the alley and yelled at him. "You take a break, Little Chef. I'm not your puppet." Then he went inside.

144

Remy decided that his family and friends had been right. To humans—even Linguini—he'd always be a rat. Remy was so angry he brought the rats to the restaurant that night to take some food.

Just then, Linguini walked into the kitchen and started to apologize to Remy. But when he saw all the rats stealing food, he got mad. "I thought you were my friend!" he cried. "Get out!"

But Remy knew his friend needed his help to cook the big meal for Ego. He also knew that he didn't want to live a lie anymore. The next day he walked into the kitchen without hiding. The other chefs saw him. "Rat!" they shrieked.

"Don't touch him!" Linguini cried. "This rat—he's the cook."

The other chefs looked at Linguini in shock. Then Remy hopped up onto Linguini's head and began tugging his hair, to show the other chefs how he got Linguini to chop and stir.

The chefs were shocked and disgusted. None of them wanted to work with a rat. They all quit.

Without any help, Linguini didn't see how he was going to be able to keep the restaurant open and serve Ego.

Luckily, the rats saw what Remy had done and knew how much he wanted to be a chef. They washed themselves off and began to help him cook. "I'm proud of you," Django told his son.

The rats did everything Remy told them. Together they cooked a special dish called ratatouille. Ego loved it and asked to meet the chef. When the critic realized Remy had cooked the meal, he left. But the next morning, the review in the newspaper said Remy was the best chef in Paris—without revealing he was a rat. Gusteau had always said "anyone can cook" and Remy had proven him right.

So what did Remy do next? He and Linguini opened a new restaurant named La Ratatouille. There, the rats had their very own place to eat. Linguini was the maitre d'—he liked it much better than cooking—and Remy was a real chef at last!

The Shadow Game

Andy loved going to Cowboy Camp, and one summer he decided to take his *Woody's Roundup* toys with him. The first night, while all of the campers were asleep, the Roundup gang gathered around a small campfire. They'd decided to sleep under the stars. The Prospector wrapped himself in a sleeping bag, put his cowboy hat on his belly, and closed his eyes. "Good night," he mumbled.

But Jessie the cowgirl didn't want to go to sleep. "Let's play a shadow game," she said excitedly. She jumped up. "Whoever makes the scariest shadow wins!"

Woody and his horse, Bullseye, thought the game sounded like fun.

150

The Prospector began to snore.

Jessie giggled. "Who wants to start?" she asked. "I think the Prospector's busy."

"Ladies first," Woody replied.

"*Yeeeeehah!*" Jessie exclaimed.

The Prospector woke with a start. "Pipe down!" he cried. "I'm trying to get some shut-eye."

"Sorry," Jessie apologized. Then she turned back to Bullseye and Woody. She flapped her arms up and down. "Look, I'm a bat. Nah, that's too easy. I'll come up with something better."

A few minutes later, Jessie motioned Bullseye toward the fire. She put her hands in a fist and curled up her index fingers.

"Why, it's a longhorn steer!" Woody exclaimed, pointing to Bullseye's face.

"That's right, pardner," Jessie answered.

Next, it was Bullseye's turn. The horse thought for a moment. Then he leaped up and yanked the hat off Woody's head.

"Hey!" the cowboy cried. "Why would you do a thing like that?"

Then Jessie figured it out. Bullseye wasn't being rude, he was making a shadow!

"It's a mountain lion, Woody," she explained.

"Would you look at that? You're right," the cowboy said. "Good one, Bullseye!"

"Now it's my turn," Woody said. "Hold on." He got up and ran off.

A minute later, he returned with a stick. He took his hat back from Bullseye and walked toward a large rock. "*Sssss*," he hissed.

"*Oooh*, a serpent," Jessie said. "That's more frightening than the mountain lion. But I bet I can do one that's even scarier." She tied a couple of sticks to her boot and made a shadow of a monster. "*Rrrrrrrrr*," she roared.

Bullseye got so frightened, he whinnied loudly and hid behind a rock.

The Prospector awoke with a start! He saw Jessie's shadow and jumped up in fright. "Yikes!" he cried. "What's happening?"

"We were playing a spooky shadows game," said Jessie, laughing.

"And you just made the best one!" Woody cried.

Nemo and the Surprise Party

One day, Nemo, a little clown fish, was telling his dad, Marlin, about something their good friend Dory had done.

"You know," said Marlin, "Dory's birthday is coming up. She mentioned it a while ago. But you know her—she's probably forgotten all about it."

Nemo decided he wanted to do something special for Dory. After all, she was like family. I know, he thought, I'll throw her a surprise birthday party!

At recess the next day, Nemo asked his friends, Pearl the octopus, Tad the butterfly fish, and Sheldon the sea horse to help plan Dory's party.

"Count me in," said Pearl.

"Me, too," Sheldon agreed.

"I love parties!" Tad exclaimed.

"Then let's meet right after school and start planning," Nemo suggested.

That afternoon, the friends met near the sponge beds. Soon they were having a contest to see who could bounce the highest. After they declared Pearl the winner, they got down to work.

"What kind of food should we have at Dory's party?" asked Nemo.

"Kelp cake and algae ice cream," Sheldon replied.

"What about sea-plant pizza?" asked Tad. "And salty seawater punch?"

"I'm getting hungry already," said Nemo. "Now what should we do about music? I wish we knew a band."

"*We* could be the band," said Pearl. "I'm great on the sand-dollar tambourines."

"Yeah, and I play the clamshell drums," said Sheldon.

"Great!" cried Nemo. "And Tad could strum some kelp while I play the conch shell. Let's meet here tomorrow after school to practice."

Back at their anemone home that evening, Nemo told
Marlin about the party.

Marlin looked a little worried for a moment. Then he
reminded himself how resourceful Nemo was. He smiled at his
son. "That's a big project," he said. "But if you put your mind to
it, I'm sure you can do it."

"I can, Dad!" Nemo said confidently. "Dory's surprise party is
going to be the best ever. Just wait and see."

The next day, Nemo and his friends were swimming toward the sponge beds with their musical instruments when they bumped into Dory.

"Hi Mimo! Hi kids!" Dory exclaimed. She had trouble remembering anything, especially Nemo's name. "What are you up to?"

"Er . . . umm," Nemo stammered.

"Music-class homework," Tad piped up.

"Well, have fun," said Dory, swimming off in the other direction.

The friends smiled at each other and began to practice. At first, they didn't sound very good. But after a while, they began to hit their groove.

After school, the next afternoon, Nemo and his friends talked about who to invite to the party.

"What about Crush and Squirt?" Sheldon suggested. "Sea turtles sure know how to have a good time."

"Everyone from school, including Mr. Ray," said Tad.

"And I'll invite Bruce, Anchor, and Chum," Nemo said.

"Those sharks will make everyone nervous," said Pearl. "But, if they're friends of Dory's, I suppose we should invite them."

"Let's give them a job so they stay out of trouble," said Nemo. "Like serving the punch. Okay, I think we're all set."

Tad, Pearl, Sheldon, and Nemo swam off to invite the guests.

Finally, it was the day of the party! Nemo and his friends woke up early and started decorating. Pearl talked some starfish into making a pretty pattern on a large piece of coral. Tad and Sheldon strung seaweed streamers everywhere. Then Nemo suggested they practice singing "Happy Birthday."

The four friends began to sing. Just as they finished the line "Happy Birthday, dear Dory," they heard another voice join in. It was Dory!

"I love singing!" she exclaimed. "How did you know it was my birthday?"

"You told me," said Nemo.

"Really, Pluto?" asked Dory, "I don't remember that."

167

"Now the surprise is ruined," said Nemo, sadly.

"What?" said Dory. "Someone ruined your surprise? Just tell me who did it. I'll fix things."

"You mean you've forgotten already?" asked Nemo.

"Forgotten what?" Dory replied.

"Nothing," said Nemo, cracking a smile. It sure was helpful that Dory's memory wasn't very good.

"See you later," said Dory, swimming away. "Who was that birthday fish anyway?" she muttered to herself. "I think it was someone really nice, someone I really liked. . . ."

"Another close call," said Nemo to his friends. "But I think we're all set. Why don't we go home and get ready? I'll meet you guys back here with Dory."

"Nemo, I don't know if I can come to the party," said Sheldon. "My dad wants me to watch the babies."

"Bring them along," said Nemo. "The more, the merrier."

A few hours later, the guests arrived. They all hid and waited to surprise Dory. When Dory and Nemo swam in, everyone popped out of their hiding places and shouted, "Surprise!"

"Look, Pluto, it's a party for you!" Dory cried.

"No, Dory, it's for you," Nemo said. "It's your birthday."

"It is?" asked Dory. "Oh, yeah. Cool, a party for me!"

The guests cheered. Dory smiled and blushed.

Nemo led everyone in singing "Happy Birthday." Dory joined in and sang the loudest.

"You're the best friends a fish could have," said Dory. Later, she swam over to Marlin and Nemo. "I sure am glad your dad and I found you, Nemo. This is the best birthday I've ever had."

"Hey, Dory," said Nemo. "You remembered my name."

"What's that, Flipper?" asked Dory.

"Oh, nothing," Nemo said with a sigh. "Let's get some food."

"Salty seawater punch!" exclaimed Dory. "My favorite."

"Allow me to pour you some," said Bruce, the great white shark, as he flashed Dory a giant toothy grin.

"Why, thank you, sir," replied Dory.

"Happy birthday, Dory," said Chum. "You sure have a lot of food—I mean friends—here today."

"Fish are friends, not food," Anchor reminded the other two sharks.

"That's right, guys," said Dory. "Don't forget it. Hey, how about we all get some birthday cake?" They swam away.

The minute the sharks left, the other sea creatures swam over to get some punch.

Right about then, Nemo and his friends played their first song, which got everyone dancing. Even Marlin swayed a little to the melody. Later, Crush and his son Squirt whirled around to the music until they were so dizzy they had to take a break.

Crush saw Marlin and swam over to say hello. "Hey, good to see you. That son of yours is awesome, dude. This is a super party—and I've been to quite a few."

Dory couldn't remember any dance moves, so she just made them up as she went along. The sharks even shook a fin or two. Then Mr. Ray led everyone in a line dance. Nemo and the band took a break to join in.

Everyone had a lot of fun, but after a few hours it was time to go home. Nemo thanked Pearl, Tad, and Sheldon as they were leaving. "I couldn't have done it without you guys," he said.

"Boy," said Dory, "that birthday fish is lucky to have so many good friends."

"That lucky fish is you, Dory," Nemo reminded her.

"Oh, right, Mimo," Dory replied. "My memory just isn't very good. I think it's getting worse as I get older—or is it getting better? I can't remember. Anyway, let me thank you before I forget. This is the best birthday I've ever had." Then Dory swam on her way. "Happy birthday to me," she sang.

"You did a great job with Dory's surprise birthday party," Marlin told Nemo. "I'm proud of you."

"Thanks, Dad," said Nemo. "I was thinking we should start planning my birthday party. It's only nine months away. Have you worked on the guest list yet?"

"I hadn't really . . ." Marlin started.

"Could we have a seaweed cake? It's the best kind. What do you think, Dad?" asked Nemo.

"Son," said Marlin. "If you're planning it, I'm sure your birthday party will be the best one ever."

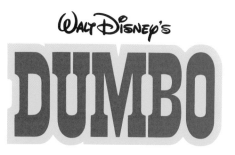

Walt Disney's DUMBO

A Brand-New Act

Camels, horses, elephants, and bears stepped out of the circus train as it pulled into town. The big-top tent went up, and performers began to practice. Everyone was busy getting ready for the circus's first show.

Everyone, that is, except Dumbo the Flying Elephant. He just watched quietly.

"Hey, Dumbo, why so glum?" Timothy Mouse asked. He paused. "Oh, I know," he said. "You're tired of your act, aren't you? I suppose you want to try something new—something more exciting."

Dumbo nodded. He and Timothy stepped into the tent. They saw pretty white horses rehearsing their act. Dumbo loved watching the horses prance around the ring in their fancy headdresses and saddles.

"I think you'd be good at this," Timothy told his elephant friend. "You could be Dumbo the Elegant Elephant."

Timothy fastened a saddle and a bridle and feather onto Dumbo. "Now just keep your head up," he instructed. "You'll be great."

Dumbo stepped into the ring with the horses.

The circus monkeys had followed Dumbo into the tent. They thought the elephant looked silly marching with the horses, so they started giggling.

Dumbo didn't pay any attention to them. He just focused on the act. But after a few minutes, he tripped over his ears and fell. The elephant looked at Timothy Mouse and shrugged.

"Don't worry, Dumbo," the mouse said. "We'll find a new act that's more your style."

181

Dumbo and Timothy went outside and spotted the lion tamer coaxing a lion through a ring of fire.

"Hey! How about Dumbo the Fearless Elephant?" Timothy suggested. "I like the sound of that!

"Come on, Dumbo. Let's try it," Timothy continued. "Don't worry, we won't use fire until we're good at it," he added.

Dumbo walked into the tent and climbed into the ring. He was eager to try another act. The circus monkeys decided to have some fun with Dumbo. They dressed up in firefighter costumes and made their way toward the ring.

"Jump straight through the hoop," coached Timothy.

Dumbo ran toward the hoop and leaped. But his ears were so large that he got stuck.

"Oh, dear!" Timothy cried. "It's a good thing we didn't use fire after all!"

As soon as the monkeys heard the word "fire," they rushed over to Dumbo and sprayed him with the hose.

"Don't worry, Dumbo," Timothy said. "We'll find a brand-new act for you."

The two friends went back to another ring inside the tent and watched the trapeze artists swing above them.

"Your ears won't get in the way here!" Timothy exclaimed. "Dumbo the Acrobatic Elephant has a nice ring to it—don't you think?"

After the performers were done, Dumbo flew to the platform and grabbed a trapeze.

"One, two, three—*go!*" Timothy shouted.

As Dumbo swung through the air, Timothy pushed a second trapeze toward him.

The little elephant caught it with his trunk. But now he was stuck in midair, holding trapezes that swung from opposite sides of the ring!

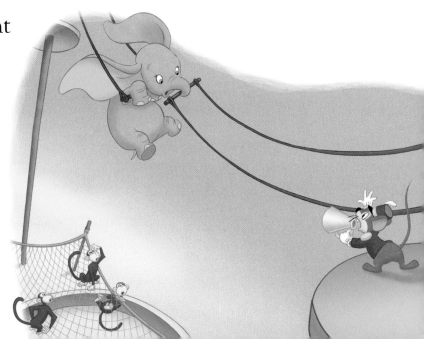

"Let go of one trapeze!" Timothy yelled.

But Dumbo seemed confused.

"Let go!" the mouse repeated.

Suddenly—much to Timothy's alarm—Dumbo let go of both trapezes at the same time!

He fell toward the net below. When he landed, the net sank way, way down. Then—*whoosh!*—Dumbo bounced way, way up and sailed toward the top of the tent. The monkeys shrieked with laughter.

When Dumbo reached the top of the tent, he began to fly!

"Way to go!" Timothy called as the elephant flew toward him. The monkeys cheered.

A few minutes later, Dumbo spotted the bear family entering the ring.

The youngest bear was learning a new act, too. He was trying to roll a barrel while balancing on it.

It wasn't easy, but at last he succeeded!

Then, Timothy and Dumbo watched as the entire bear family rehearsed their act. The bears juggled while they rode unicycles! It looked like lots of fun!

Timothy stroked his chin thoughtfully. "I bet you could do this. You could be Dumbo the Balancing Elephant!"

So Dumbo hopped on a unicycle. At first, he was a little wobbly. Then, with patience and the advice of his friend, he got his balance and began to pedal.

Dumbo rode proudly across the ring. But he was so excited about getting the hang of it that he forgot to watch where he was going. He was headed straight toward the snack bar!

"Dumbo! Look out!" Timothy shouted.

Dumbo didn't know how to stop, though. *Bam!* The unicycle hit the side of the ring.

The little elephant sailed through the air and landed in the snack bar with a crash!

Dumbo wasn't hurt, but he was covered in cotton candy! The monkeys thought he looked extremely funny.

"Oh, dear," Timothy fussed, trying to wipe off the mess. "You need a good bath. Hurry—it's almost showtime."

Dumbo went to clean up in a tub just outside the tent. The band began to rehearse, and one of the monkeys stuck a banana in a tuba.

When the tuba player blew a note, the banana flew out, and another monkey caught it.

Dumbo and Timothy saw what had happened and couldn't stop laughing. Then the little elephant had an idea.

When the band left to change into their uniforms, Dumbo filled his trunk with soapy water and poured it into the band's instruments.

The band returned shortly after and began to play as they marched into the circus ring.

"Time to put on your costume, Dumbo," Timothy said. "Your act is right after the band plays the opening number."

Dumbo and Timothy watched the band begin to play. With every note, bubbles poured out of the instruments. The audience went crazy!

Then Dumbo filled his trunk with soapy water again and flew into the circus ring.

The audience cheered wildly as he soared over them. He blew bubbles until the circus tent was filled with them. The children loved the act. They clapped and waved and tried to catch the bubbles.

"Wow!" Timothy exclaimed when Dumbo's performance was over. "You're Dumbo the Flying Elephant—with Bubbles! I think you've finally found an act that's just your style!"

Dumbo smiled happily. It was a great way to end the day.

A Day to Remember

Last year, Chicken Little's life had changed forever. He'd thought the sky was falling and had warned the people of Oakey Oaks, causing a panic. Then, when nothing happened, people got mad at him. Now everyone called him "a crazy little chicken." But Chicken Little had had enough.

As he headed for the school bus, he decided that he was going to make a change. "Today is a new day," he told himself. But things didn't seem to be going Chicken Little's way. A bunch of kids ran toward the bus and knocked him over. Before he could get up, the bus drove off.

Chicken Little leaped up and ran after the bus. He could see his classmates Foxy Loxy and Goosey Loosey watching him. With a nasty smirk, Foxy tipped a bag full of acorns out the window. *Whoa!* Chicken Little slipped on the rolling acorns and fell flat on his back. Foxy, Goosey, and the other kids laughed as the bus sped away.

Chicken Little dashed down the sidewalk and started to cross the street. But he wasn't watching where he was going. *Squish!* He stepped on a piece of gum. He tried to move, but the gum was too sticky.

Suddenly, the light turned green. The cars were headed straight for Chicken Little! Quickly, he pulled a lollipop from his pocket and licked it. Then he slapped the lollipop onto a car's rear bumper and held on tight. The car yanked him out of the gum, but his pants had stuck to the ground!

Determined to get to school, Chicken Little jumped from the car and dashed from one clump of bushes to the next. He was in his underwear, after all. When he finally arrived, he realized he couldn't just walk in the front door without any pants.

Then Chicken Little noticed a soda machine and had an idea. He got a bottle of soda, shook it as hard as he could, then tied it to his back. When he took the cap off, the fizzy soda shot him into the air like a rocket. Chicken Little flew through an open window and landed on the gym floor. He'd made it! Now all he had to do was find a pair of pants.

A little while later, Chicken Little hurried into gym class wearing a pair of origami pants he'd cleverly made out of his math homework. The class was playing dodgeball.

As Chicken Little played, he told his friends, Abby, Runt, and Fish, about his plan to do something so great that everyone would forget about the "sky is falling" incident.

Suddenly, Foxy Loxy smacked Abby in the face with a ball.

"That does it!" Chicken Little said to Foxy. "We've had enough of your bullying. Apologize right now."

Instead, Foxy's sidekick, Goosey, grabbed Chicken Little and threw him across the room. *Splat!* He hit the window. As he started to fall, he grabbed a handle on the wall.

Riiiiiiiinnngg! He'd pulled the fire alarm. Sprinklers went off, soaking everything in sight. Chicken Little's origami pants filled with water until—*rrrriipp!*—they tore and slid off. Chicken Little had lost his pants for the second time that day.

When the principal found out, he called Chicken Little's father, Buck Cluck. Chicken Little sat on a bench outside the principal's office, listening.

"Ever since that 'sky is falling' incident, he's been nothing but trouble," Principal Fetchit told Buck. "Now, you know I have the utmost respect for you. We haven't had a baseball star like you in twenty years. But let's face the facts, your kid is nothing like you. Things had better change soon . . . or else."

"Okay, thank you for talking to me," Buck replied sadly. "I'll take care of my son."

As Chicken Little listened, he stared unhappily at a case full of baseball trophies that Buck had helped win. Chicken Little wished he could make his dad proud of him.

On the drive home, Chicken Little said, "Dad? I was thinking . . . what if I joined the baseball team?"

Buck was so surprised, he nearly crashed the car. "Baseball?" he said. "Are you sure?"

"You were such a big baseball star in high school," Chicken Little replied, "I figured you could give me some pointers."

Buck wasn't so sure. After all, Chicken Little was such a tiny chicken. "Just please try not to get your hopes too high," he told his son.

Chicken Little was determined to be a great baseball player. His friends helped him train every day. But it was no use. No matter how much Chicken Little practiced, the coach wouldn't let him play.

Game after game, Chicken Little sat on the bench, while Foxy Loxy, the team's star player, scored home runs. Chicken Little tried not to get discouraged, but how was he going to make his dad proud if he never got the chance?

Finally, it was the last game of the season. Chicken Little's team, the Oakey Oaks Acorns, was up against their old rivals, the Spud Valley Taters.

The Acorns gave it their all, but by the ninth inning, the injuries had mounted, and they were down by one run. Then, Goosey Loosey got on base. A good hit could get her home and tie the game—but they'd still need another run to win. The game was on the line, and there were only two batters left: Chicken Little and Foxy Loxy.

The announcer looked at the lineup card. "Up next, Chicken Little," he said.

The crowd was furious. "He's going to lose the game for us! Put in Foxy!" one dad shouted.

No one expected Chicken Little to even try to hit the ball. If he let four balls go by, he could walk to first base, and the coach would put Foxy in to try and win the game.

Everyone watching held their breath as the little chicken stepped up to the plate.

The pitcher threw the first pitch. Chicken Little swung at the ball—after it had already landed in the catcher's mitt. The crowd gasped. "Strike one!" called the umpire.

"Boooo!" said the crowd.

The pitcher threw the second pitch. And Chicken Little missed again. "Strike two!" cried the ump.

The pitcher wound up for the third pitch. If Chicken Little missed this ball, the Acorns would lose the game.

"Today is a new day," Chicken Little told himself. As the ball came toward him, he closed his eyes and swung his bat hard.

Craaack!

Chicken Little's eyes flew open. He'd hit the ball!

Chicken Little was so surprised, he just stood there. "Go, son! Run! Run!" Buck yelled from the bleachers. At last, Chicken Little began to run—the wrong way! "The other way!" his dad called.

Finally, Chicken Little figured out which way to run. Luckily, the other team hadn't been ready for the hit. To the crowd's astonishment, Chicken Little passed first base, second base, third base . . .

Chicken Little slid into home just as the throw came from the outfield. After the umpire dusted off the plate, he saw Chicken Little's foot and made the call. "The runner is safe!"

The crowd went wild. Chicken Little had won the game!

At home later that night, Buck and Chicken Little replayed the victory. "The mighty Acorns win!" they cried, dancing around the room.

"I guess that puts the whole 'sky is falling' incident behind us," said Buck.

Chicken Little was thrilled. His plan had worked, and he'd made his dad proud. Maybe, he thought, things were finally changing after all.

It had been a long day, and Chicken Little knew he'd sleep well that night. After all, one of his dreams had just come true.

Disney's ARISTOCATS

The Coziest Carriage

One day, O'Malley and Duchess took the kittens to visit their dear friend, Scat Cat. O'Malley had lived in the same neighborhood as Scat Cat back when they were both alley cats.

But then O'Malley had met Duchess and her kittens, Berlioz, Toulouse, and Marie. He'd liked them so much he'd decided to become part of their family. They all lived in a grand mansion with their kindly owner, Madame Bonfamille. Even though he'd moved, O'Malley liked to go visit his old pals.

Scat Cat lived in a junkyard, in a broken-down carriage that had once been very grand. Now the spokes on the wheels were damaged, and there was an enormous hole in the roof.

Still, as far as Scat Cat was concerned, it could not have been more perfect. "I feel free here," he told the kittens. "I can come and go as I please. And when I stretch out on the cushions at night, I look up and there are the stars a-twinklin' back at me!"

The kittens had a grand time playing with Scat Cat in the junkyard. But when the sun went down, they were glad to return to the soft pillows, cozy blankets, and warm milk at Madame Bonfamille's.

A few days later, Scat Cat appeared at Madame's doorstep.

"My carriage is missing!" he explained to his friends. "I went into town to stretch my legs, and when I got back—*poof!*—the carriage was gone!"

"You will have to stay with us," said Duchess. "I'm sure Madame would be delighted to have you as our guest."

"Oh, goody!" the kittens cheered.

"You'll love it here," said Berlioz.

"Well," Scat Cat said, thinking it over, "that's a mighty nice invitation. Don't mind if I do." He plopped into an armchair. "Huh, no ripped cushions here!"

The kittens scampered up next to him. "Of course not," Marie said, "Madame would never allow worn-out chairs in her house. Only the best furniture will do."

Scat Cat nodded. "I guess everyone just has a different idea of what 'best' is, little lady. Me, I prefer cushions with the stuffing coming out of them. But who knows, maybe I'll get used to this."

"Would you like to paint with me?" Toulouse asked.

"How about I play a little piano music?" volunteered Berlioz.

"Or you could sing with me," Marie offered.

"Now, now, children," Duchess said. "Scat Cat just arrived. Let him settle in a bit."

But after just one night, Scat Cat didn't know if he *would* settle in. The life of a house cat just wasn't for him.

Everything at Madame Bonfamille's happened on a schedule. Meals were at eight o'clock, noon, and six o'clock, sharp. Naps were from nine to eleven, and one to four. Outings took place at 4:30. The rest of the time was spent in the house or in Madame's small, walled garden. The old cat was used to coming and going as he pleased.

"Do you know what I miss most?" Scat Cat said with a sigh. "My old carriage. What I wouldn't give to be able to look up at the sky and count the twinklin' stars as I drift off to sleep on those lumpy, worn-out cushions. . . ."

It was hard for the kittens to imagine how any cat could like a broken-down carriage better than a soft, cozy bed. But that's what Scat Cat had come to love, and that was good enough for them.

"I just wish there was some way we could get that carriage back for him," Marie said.

"Maybe there is!" Berlioz said with a grin. "Follow me!"

He led the kittens to the drawing room where their mother was relaxing.

"Can we go to the carriage house, Mama?" Berlioz asked.

"Well," their mother replied, "you are supposed to be practicing your Italian this afternoon."

"But it's for a special surprise for Scat Cat," Toulouse said.

"All right, then," Duchess said, "but just for a while."

A few minutes later, the kittens were inside Madame's carriage house. For some time now, Madame had been complaining about her old carriage. "It's not even worth repairing," she had said one day.

With this in mind, Berlioz climbed into the carriage, unfurled his claws, and gleefully pounced on the old upholstery.

"Come on—dig in!" he said gleefully.

Toulouse and Marie joined him, and in no time the kittens had those cushions looking like the ones in Scat Cat's old carriage.

"Don't forget the roof!" Marie reminded her brothers. The kittens raced up to the top of the carriage, where they jumped and bounced to their hearts' content. Finally, after a triple backward somersault, Toulouse came crashing through the carriage roof, making a hole the size of Madame's parasol.

"Hooray!" cheered Marie.

Just then, Madame walked in. She looked at the carriage and smiled. "It's worse than I remember. At last I have an excuse to buy a new one," she said. "Take this carriage away at once."

That evening, the kittens got permission to take Scat Cat to the junkyard. "I don't believe it!" Scat Cat exclaimed when they showed him his new home there. "The seats are even more torn up than the ones in my old carriage. And look at that hole in the roof. It's *purr-fect!* How can I ever thank you?"

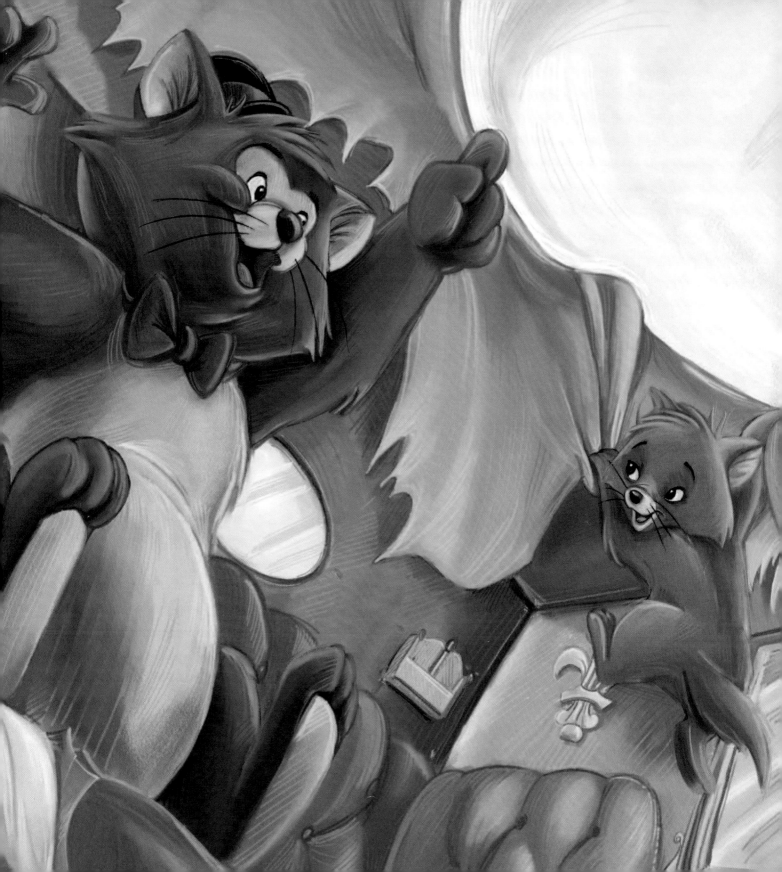

"Just promise you'll come back to visit us again," Berlioz told him. "And maybe have a little warm milk on hand when we come to see you."

"It's a deal," Scat Cat replied.

The kittens visited with their friend until the moon began to rise. Then they waved good-bye and headed home to snuggle beneath their cozy blankets.

In his new carriage, Scat Cat looked at the stars and smiled contentedly before drifting off to sleep.

Walt Disney's Sleeping Beauty

Aurora's Slumber Party

Princess Aurora loved being married to Prince Phillip and living at the castle. But she missed her friends Flora, Fauna, and Merryweather. They were the fairies who'd raised her in a cottage in the woods to protect her from an evil spell and were like aunts to her.

One day, Phillip told her he had to visit another kingdom for a couple of days. "Why don't you have friends over while I'm away?" he suggested.

"That's a wonderful idea!" Aurora replied. "I'll invite them to a slumber party."

The princess worked all evening making invitations. She sent them out the very next day.

Flora, Fauna, and Merryweather were quite excited when they got their invitations. The fairies arrived at the castle that night with their wands, ready to use their magic.

"We don't need magic to have fun," said Aurora. "There are all kinds of things to do. But first, you need to change into your nightgowns! This is a slumber party, after all!"

A little while later, the fairies began to get hungry. "I'll use a spell to make some food," said Merryweather.

"We have bread, butter, strawberries, and cream right here," Aurora pointed out. "You can make yourself a wonderful snack without using magic."

"This is fun!" Merryweather exclaimed as she made herself a triple-decker berry sandwich. It looked so good, the other fairies raced over to make their own. When Flora bit into hers, a dollop of cream flew across the room, right onto Aurora's face!

"Oops," Flora said. "I'm sorry, Princess."

But Aurora wasn't upset. In fact, it made her giggle. Soon everyone was laughing. The party was off to a great start.

"Come over here, everyone!" Aurora called. "It's time for a talent show. Who wants to begin?"

Merryweather decided to go first. She pulled out her wand and pointed it at herself. Suddenly, her nightgown started changing colors. First it was blue, then it was pink, then it was orange.

"No, no, no!" Aurora cried. The fairies stared at her in surprise. "What I mean to say is, that looks wonderful, but let's not use magic."

The fairies were puzzled. "But our magic *is* our talent," Fauna said.

"It's not your only talent, though," Aurora insisted. She grabbed Fauna by the hand and began to sing and dance. Soon the fairy was whirling around the room with her.

"Hurrah!" Flora and Merryweather cheered.

Then Flora ended the show with a lively dance routine of her own.

A little later, Fauna had an idea. "Let's make a surprise for the morning," she suggested.

"I don't want to do anything that's going to take a long time," Merryweather grumbled.

"Why don't we make some cinnamon rolls?" Aurora offered. They gathered ingredients and began to make the dough.

While they waited for the dough to rise, the princess suggested they do something else. The friends went upstairs, and Flora grabbed a pillow and swung it at Aurora. The princess ducked and grabbed a pillow of her own.

A few minutes later, feathers covered the room and Aurora and the fairies were out of breath from laughing. "It's probably time to finish the rolls," Aurora said.

She and the fairies went down to the kitchen and saw that the ball of dough had become the size of a table! "What could have happened?" Aurora cried.

"I may have used a teensy bit of magic," Merryweather admitted. "I just wanted to finish up quickly."

"That's all right," Aurora said with a yawn. "We'll have enough for the whole kingdom."

Fauna pulled her wand out. "I think a little more magic would make this a lot faster." A few minutes later, all the rolls were done.

Aurora and the fairies went back upstairs. "Let's read a story," the princess suggested. Flora began to read and after a few minutes, everyone was sleepy.

"This has been a wonderful slumber party," Aurora said. "Thanks for coming. Good night, fairies."

"Good night, Princess," the fairies replied. And very soon, they all drifted off to sleep.

Winnie the Pooh

Piglet's Night-Lights

It was twilight in the Hundred-Acre Wood when Winnie the Pooh knocked on his good friend Piglet's door. Pooh was carrying a backpack with an enormous pot of honey sticking out of the top.

"Ready for our campout, Piglet?" Pooh called.

Piglet opened the door and looked around anxiously. "Are you really quite sure about this, Pooh?" he asked. "It's getting awfully dark out there, and it's so light and cozy in here. Maybe we could just camp out in my living room."

"That would be a camp-*in*, not a camp-*out*," Pooh said. He reminded Piglet that their friends would be going, too.

Piglet smiled nervously.

Pooh offered to help Piglet get ready. He stuffed haycorn muffins into Piglet's backpack while Piglet neatly packed his favorite blanket and teddy bear.

"I have the feeling I'm forgetting something," Piglet said.

"Well, let's see," Pooh said. "We have honey." He patted the sticky honeypot in his pack. "And we have plenty of muffins." Just to be sure, Pooh tucked two more next to Piglet's teddy bear. "What else could we possibly need?"

241

Pooh and Piglet started toward the campsite. As they walked, it got darker and darker, and Piglet got more and more frightened. "What's that?" he asked suddenly, pointing to a scary-looking shape in the trees.

"I'm not certain, Piglet," Pooh answered. He was beginning to get a bit nervous himself. "Maybe if we close our eyes, it will go away." He and Piglet shut their eyes and stood very still for a few minutes.

"Hello down there!" called a voice from above. Pooh and Piglet both jumped, startled.

"Who's there?" Pooh asked, trembling as he looked up at the trees. All he could see were two eyes staring down at them.

"Why, it's me—Owl," the voice answered. "I thought you two might need a little help finding the others. We owls can see quite well at night, you know."

"Oh, thank you, Owl!" Piglet said.

By the time the friends reached the campsite, it was completely dark. Pooh bumped into Rabbit, who was struggling to put up the tent.

"Well, don't just stand there," Rabbit said. "I need all the help I can get!"

"Did I hear someone say 'help'?" Tigger called, bouncing into the clearing. "Have no fear, Tigger's here—with illuminagination!" he said proudly, holding up a lantern.

"Oh, and you brought a light, too!" cried Piglet, peeking out from under the hood of his jacket. "Thank goodness—it's awfully dark out here."

245

With the lantern lighting the area, the friends set up the tent. Piglet climbed inside and began to unpack. A few minutes later, he poked his head back out. "Oh, no!" he wailed. "I forgot my night-light! I can't sleep without one." He wrung his hands. "What am I going to do?"

"Don't worry, Buddy Boy," Tigger said. "You can use my lantern as a night-light!" Just then, the lantern flickered out.

"On second thought," Tigger said, diving into the tent to dig through Rabbit's bag, "Long Ears must have something in here you can use."

Tigger found a kite, a flowerpot, and kitchen pans. He pulled them out and saw garden tools and a ball. Finally, at the very bottom, he spotted a flashlight.

Tigger tried to turn it on, but nothing happened. "This thingamabob's not working either!" he cried.

At that moment, there was a crash in the nearby bushes. "Look who we found!" Pooh exclaimed. He pointed to Eeyore, who was standing next to Rabbit and Owl.

Eeyore looked around. "Can't have a campout without a campfire," he said.

Everyone agreed wholeheartedly. They went to gather some sticks, and a few minutes later a cheerful fire was burning.

"Campfires certainly are pleasant," Piglet said. "They make a very good sort of light."

"They do a fantalicious job cooking marshy-mallows, too!" Tigger cried, wrestling with a particularly gooey marshmallow.

"Fire is fine," Rabbit said. "But I think sunlight is the best light of all—it makes my vegetables grow."

"I like the way the sun warms my tummy when I lie in the grass," Pooh said.

"And the colors at sunset are splendid," Piglet added.

"Look at that shadow on the tent!" Tigger interrupted.

"That looks like your tail to me," Rabbit said.

"Well, what do you know!" Tigger replied.

"Guess what this is?" Rabbit asked, fluttering his hands like a butterfly.

Tigger and Owl looked at the tent. A shape was moving on it.

"Why, it's a shadow puppet!" Owl declared.

The friends played shadow puppets until bedtime. Then almost everyone went to bed. Piglet wouldn't leave the light of the fire, though. Pooh decided to keep him company.

After a short while, the fire began to fade. "Maybe we should go to sleep now, Piglet," Pooh said, yawning.

"I can't sleep without a night-light, Pooh," Piglet replied.

Pooh tapped his forehead to wake up any ideas that might be there. "Think, think, think," he said.

Looking up at the night sky, Pooh thought of something. "The stars are night-lights, Piglet," he said, pointing up at the sparkling stars.

Just then a firefly landed right between Pooh's eyes. Crossing his eyes to see it, Pooh tumbled backward off the log he was sitting on.

"And so are the fireflies," he added.

Piglet looked around. "You're right, Pooh!" he cried. "There are night-lights everywhere!"

Piglet pointed to the moon. "Look how bright the moon is tonight," he said. "It's even brighter than my own night-light. I feel much better."

"Do you think you might be able to sleep now, Piglet?" Pooh asked with a huge yawn. "Piglet?"

But Piglet didn't answer. He was already fast asleep.

MICKEY MOUSE

MICKEY MOUSE
AND THE PET SHOP

Mickey Mouse was a great friend of Mr. Palmer, who owned the local pet shop. One day, Mr. Palmer had to go on an overnight trip. He couldn't leave the animals by themselves, so he asked Mickey to watch the shop while he was gone.

"I will be back tomorrow afternoon," said Mr. Palmer as he waved good-bye. "You shouldn't have any problems."

"Have a good time," called Mickey. "This will be a snap!"

"A snap!" a parrot repeated.

Mickey decided to get to know the animals. So he walked around, gazing at the colorful fish, talking parrots, furry kittens, and cuddly dogs. They all seemed content—except for a cute little puppy who wouldn't stop whimpering.

"Poor little fella," said Mickey. "What you need is some attention." He lifted the puppy from the kennel.

The puppy wriggled out of Mickey's arms and raced over to the fishbowl for a drink of water.

"Watch out!" screeched the parrot. "Watch out!"

He was too late. The puppy knocked over the bowl and the fish went flying across the store.

"Gotcha!" Mickey called as he caught the fish and put it in a new fishbowl. Then he put the puppy back in the kennel. "Now you can't cause any more trouble," he said.

Just then, the door opened. It was Mickey's first customer! He was so excited that he forgot to lock the kennel door.

"Can I help you?" Mickey asked.

Before the customer could answer, the puppy had gotten out and opened the door to a cage full of mice. Now mice were everywhere!

"*Oh my!* I'll come back later—much later!" cried the customer as she raced for the door.

After the customer left, Mickey gathered up all the pets and put them back where they belonged. This time he made sure he locked the kennel door.

"Don't worry, little guy," he said to the puppy. "Someone will buy you. You'll see." Then Mickey went upstairs for the night.

When Mickey tried to go to sleep, the puppy howled at the top of his lungs. He just wouldn't stop. Mickey tried hiding under the covers, but that didn't work. Then he tried covering his ears with a pillow. That didn't work either. Mickey didn't know what to do.

Finally, the puppy got exactly what he wanted—a cozy spot under the covers, right next to Mickey!

When Mickey woke up the next morning, the puppy was gone. Mickey looked all over the house for him, but he was nowhere to be found. Maybe he's down in the pet shop, thought Mickey. He went downstairs to check.

Mickey couldn't believe his eyes when he walked into the store. It was a mess! Books were scattered on the floor, and the plants had been turned over. But the puppy wasn't there.

Mickey got dressed and then began to look for his little friend. He was about to give up when he remembered to check the storage room. Sure enough, the puppy was there.

Mickey picked up the puppy, brought him back to the kennel, and locked the door. "Now you can't cause any more trouble."

"Well," said Mickey with a sigh. "I guess I should begin tidying up the store."

As he worked, the puppy began to whine. Mickey felt bad, so he opened the kennel door. The puppy followed him around, trying to be good. He helped Mickey put the books back, dust the counter, and sweep up the soil from the flowerpots.

"You may be a rascal," said Mickey, "but I sure am getting used to having you around."

Mickey and the puppy had just finished cleaning up when Mr. Palmer strode in.

"It looks like everything went smoothly," he said. "I hope none of the animals gave you any trouble."

"It was as easy as pie," a very tired Mickey replied.

Then Mr. Palmer handed Mickey his paycheck. "Thanks for helping me out," he said. "I hope you will come back soon."

Mickey just smiled.

As Mickey was about to leave, the puppy began to howl.

"I'm going to miss you, too, little fella," Mickey said sadly.

Suddenly Mickey had an idea. He could take the pup instead of the pay! Now everybody was happy—especially the parrot, who screeched, "And don't come back!"

"But what should I call you?" Mickey wondered aloud.

Just then, Mickey saw some pictures of outer space in a newspaper. The headline read: NEW PICTURES OF PLUTO! "That's it! I'll call you Pluto!" he exclaimed.

Pluto licked Mickey's cheek happily. From that day on, Mickey and Pluto were the best of friends.

Friday Night Fun

Lightning McQueen and his best friend, Mater the tow truck, raced to the tractor field. It was Friday night, and they were ready for some fun.

"You first, Mater," McQueen whispered when they got there.

The tow truck looked out at all the sleeping tractors. Then he quietly drove up to one and honked. *Beep! Beep!* The startled tractor woke up, tipped over, and moaned as its wheels spun helplessly in the air. Then it made the noise that Mater and McQueen loved. *Snort!* The race car and the tow truck erupted into a fit of giggles.

"Your turn, McQueen," said Mater.

McQueen smirked and snuck up next to another tractor. Since he didn't have a horn, he revved his engine. *Vroom, vroom!* The noise was so loud that every single tractor in the field woke up and tipped over. *Snort! Snort! Snort! Snort!* McQueen and Mater laughed and laughed.

"Boy, you is good," Mater said when they finally caught their breath.

"Well, I learned from the best," McQueen told him.

"Aw, shucks," answered Mater.

Suddenly, a pair of headlights shone in their faces as Sheriff pulled up in front of them. "Mater, what have I told you about tractor tipping?"

"To not to," Mater answered sheepishly.

"That's right," said Sheriff. "McQueen, you should know better, too. I'll see you both in traffic court tomorrow."

As they drove to town, Mater whispered, "That was fu-un wasn't it, buddy?"

"You bet," whispered McQueen. Still, he hoped Sally, the sporty blue Porsche he had a crush on, wouldn't find out.

The next morning, Sheriff escorted Mater and McQueen to traffic court. McQueen spotted Sally and drove over. "Didn't know you would be here," he said. "Want to be my lawyer?"

"Sorry," she replied. "The tractors hired me first."

McQueen frowned as the judge, a 1951 Hudson Hornet named Doc Hudson, entered the room.

"Listen Doc," started McQueen, "Mater and I were just doing a little harmless tractor tipping. . . ."

"Harmless!" interrupted Sally. She pointed to the row of sleeping tractors behind her. "The tractors wouldn't call it harmless. They can't even get a good night's rest because these two are always waking them up."

"Aw, we didn't mean the little fellers any harm," said Mater.

"I think the fairest thing to do," said Doc, "is to sentence you boys to community service. Why don't you help Ramone clean his shop? And no more tractor tipping!"

279

McQueen and Mater drove over to Ramone's House of Body Art. "Well, here's the job," Ramone said as he showed them the back room. It looked like it hadn't been cleaned in a while. "I'm going outside. All set?"

"You bet," answered McQueen and Mater.

A few minutes later, Mater accidentally knocked over a can of pink paint. The lid flew off, and the paint splattered McQueen.

"Hey!" McQueen hollered. "Watch it."

"Sorry," said Mater. "But you sure do look purty in pink."

"Let's see how you look in it!" shouted McQueen. He hurled an open can of paint at Mater. Then the tow truck threw lime green paint at McQueen. After a few minutes, the pair was covered in paint. When Ramone peeked in, he got splattered, too.

"I can't believe my eyes, man," cried Ramone. "Look at my shop! Out! Before I take a blowtorch to both of you!"

The friends left the shop and got Red the fire truck to hose them off. Once they were clean, they drove over to Doc's garage.

"Mater and I messed up again," said McQueen.

"Yeah," Mater agreed. "We got into a little bitty paint fight at Ramone's."

"How can we make things right?" asked McQueen.

"Boys, boys." Doc sighed. "Why don't you go help Luigi with his new shipment of tires? And, please, try to behave this time."

"Yes, sir," McQueen and Mater answered.

The two friends zipped over to Luigi's Casa Della Tires. There they found Luigi, a 1959 Fiat, and Guido, a spunky little forklift, bickering in Italian.

"Doc sent us over here to give you a hand," said McQueen.

"*Grazie,*" said Luigi. "Can you-a move those tires inside? The front of Casa Della Tires must be *bellissima* at all times."

"Might as well get started," Mater said. He passed a tire to McQueen, who put it inside. Guido and Luigi went to the showroom.

A dozen tires later, McQueen said, "There's got to be a faster way. What if we piled up the tires and pushed them inside?"

"Sure," said Mater. "Otherwise, we're gonna be here all dadgum day."

So McQueen and Mater began stacking tires. When they were ready to push the pile, it was so high that they couldn't see over it.

They were sick of working, so they moved the pile anyway. It slammed right into Luigi's Leaning Tower of Tires. All at once, the tower toppled over!

"My-a tower!" cried Luigi, zooming outside. "She is-a ruined. I can't believe it. You two break-a my heart."

Guido just shook his head and muttered in Italian.

"Sorry," McQueen said. "It was a mistake. We can fix it."

"Just go," Luigi said.

McQueen and Mater looked at the ground.

"Guess we better go see Doc . . . again," Mater said.

When the tow truck and race car arrived at Doc's, he gave them one last chance. "Go find Bessie and surprise Flo with a new paving job."

"This sure is a nice surprise," Flo said, when Mater and McQueen drove up to the V8 Café. "Since my parking lot's going to get a makeover, I'm taking the afternoon off."

"Don't you worry," said Mater. "We's getting right to work."

Mater and McQueen spent hours scraping up the old pavement in the hot sun.

"I'm just about pooped," said Mater.

"Same here," answered McQueen. "Do you think anyone would mind if we took a little break and zipped out to the butte for a little race?"

"Wee-hoo!" shouted Mater, driving off at top speed.

McQueen raced after him . . . backward. "Why are you driving so slow?" he asked, smiling.

The friends had so much fun that they forgot all about the paving job at Flo's V8 Café. By the time they remembered, it was dark. "We'll just finish it in the morning," McQueen said.

"Okay, buddy," Mater agreed.

The next morning, Mater and McQueen drove over to Flo's. Just about everyone in Radiator Springs was hard at work, trying to finish the paving job. No one had been able to drive in for their breakfast fill-up, and they were grumpy.

"Hey, man, look who finally rolled out of the garage," said Ramone.

"I can't-a believe they showed up," added Luigi.

Mater and McQueen were embarrassed. "Sorry, everyone," the race car said. "We'll take it from here."

Then Mater and McQueen got to work. McQueen worked with Bessie to do the smoothest paving job ever. A couple of hours later, they were done. The V8 Café looked fantastic.

"Thanks, boys," said Flo. "Folks, drive on up for the finest fuel in Carburetor County!"

"All breakfast fill-ups on Mater and me!" shouted McQueen. Everyone cheered.

Everything finally went back to normal in Radiator Springs . . . until Friday night rolled around again.

"Hey, buddy," whispered Mater to McQueen. "How 'bout a little tractor-tipping fun ternight?"

"I don't know, Mater," McQueen replied. "Why don't we just go to the drive-in?"

"Woo-hoo! I'd love to, little buddy," said Mater. "Race ya!"

A few minutes later, Mater and McQueen arrived at the theater. They got some refreshments and settled in for a night of fun.

Dream Tales

Deep in the forest sat a cozy little cottage where the Seven Dwarfs made their home. Doc, Happy, Grumpy, Dopey, Sleepy, Sneezy, and Bashful lived there with Snow White, a princess who had run away from her wicked stepmother.

One morning, Snow White got up early and prepared a special breakfast for the Dwarfs. The house was filled with the delicious smell of fresh cinnamon porridge. It wasn't long before every last Dwarf—even Sleepy—followed his nose from his bed to the breakfast table.

"Good morning!" Snow White greeted the Dwarfs. "Did everyone sleep well?"

"Bike a lady," Doc replied. "Er, I mean, *like a baby*. What about you, Princess?"

Snow White shook her head. "I had a bad dream," she admitted. "I dreamed that my stepmother, the wicked Queen, was coming to get me."

"Oh, no!" Happy cried. "If she's coming, you'd better hide!"

"And quick!" Grumpy added. "That Queen is trouble, mark my words!"

The other Dwarfs nodded and looked nervous. Dopey even hid under the table.

Snow White laughed. "Why are you hiding?" she exclaimed. "Why, you should know that dreams aren't real! They can't hurt you one bit." She smiled at the Dwarfs. "What about all of you? Did you dream about anything last night?"

Doc spoke first. "I dreamed I was giving a beach—er, a *peach*—that is, a *speech* in front of the entire kingdom." He shrugged sheepishly. "And for some reason, I just couldn't make the rights come out word. I mean, *the words come out right*."

Happy laughed cheerfully. "I dreamed about all the things that make me happy."

"Like what?" Snow White asked.

"Yeah, what's there to be so happy about?" Grumpy added.

Happy paused for a moment. "Friends and work and sunny days and apple dumplings . . . well, gosh, I guess all sorts of things," he replied. "Just about everything makes me smile." He giggled. "Why, even my dream made me smile!"

Just then, a butterfly flew in the open window and landed on Happy's nose. The Dwarf smiled.

"Did you dream about butterflies, too?" Doc asked.

Snow White laughed.

"As a matter of fact, I did!" Happy exclaimed.

"Oh, for Pete's sake!" Grumpy cried. "Didn't anyone have a bad dream?"

"I had a terrible dream," Sleepy said with a yawn. "I dreamed I was bone tired. But I couldn't fall asleep, no matter how hard I tried. It was awful!"

"Oh, that is terrible," Happy said. "But today's Sunday. That means you can take a nap later."

Sleepy smiled. "I like naps." He ate a spoonful of porridge and then fell asleep in his chair. He fell toward the table and— *splat!*—his face hit the bowl of porridge.

"Oh, Sleepy!" Snow White cried. "Are you all right? Maybe you should lie down for a few minutes."

Sleepy wiped the porridge off his face and climbed up the ladder and into bed.

Snow White cleared away Sleepy's bowl. "What about you, Sneezy? Did you remember your dream?"

"*Aaaa-choo!*" Sneezy sneezed. He sniffed. "I dreabed I couldn't stop sdeezing."

"Are you sure it was a dream, Sneezy?" Happy asked.

Sneezy sneezed again. *Aa-choo!* Then he nodded.

"How do you know?" Happy asked.

"Well, in my dream I kept sneezing flowers. And every time I sneezed more flowers, they made me sneeze even more," Sneezy said.

"Well, you must be awake now, then," Snow White said. "There are no flowers around anymore."

"*Aaaa-choo!*" Sneezy sneezed again. "Nope, no flowers!"

Snow White turned to Bashful. "What about you?" she asked.

Bashful rubbed his ear. "Gosh," he said, blushing. "Er, I had a dream."

"What was it about?" asked Snow White.

Bashful turned a deeper red. "I dreamed I was a brave prince." He looked down.

"And what else?" Snow White asked.

"I rode into battle and fought a fierce dragon," Bashful said shyly.

Snow White smiled. "That's wonderful!"

"Humph!" Grumpy spoke up. "A dragon? I've heard better stories than that."

Bashful looked at the floor.

"But it wasn't a story, Grumpy," Snow White said. "It was a dream."

"Bah! Dreams are a bunch of nonsense," Grumpy replied.

"I heard you talking in your sleep nast light," Doc said. "I mean *last night*." Grumpy glared at him.

Snow White smiled and scooped some cinnamon porridge into Grumpy's bowl. "Why don't you tell us about your dream?" she asked gently.

"Well, if you must know," Grumpy grumbled, "I dreamed about a pie. An apple pie. Very tasty. And I had it all to myself—no sharing!"

"Well that sounds like a lovely dream," Snow White said.

"Humph!" Grumpy retorted.

"Dopey?" Snow White said. "Did you dream about anything last night?"

Dopey shook his head, looking sheepish.

Grumpy rolled his eyes. "Of course he did," he snapped.

"Dopey has the same night every dream," Doc said. "Er, the *same dream every night.*"

Happy nodded. "He dreams he's the wisest ruler ever to sit upon a throne."

"Ooh!" Snow White said, clapping her hands. "That sounds like a marvelous dream, Dopey!"

Snow White looked around. "We've been talking all morning," she said. "I'd better get Sleepy up or he'll never sleep tonight." She climbed up the ladder.

But when she got to the Dwarfs' room, the beds were empty! Where could he be?

Then she heard someone snoring. She crouched down and peeked under the bed. Sleepy was fast asleep. She shook him gently, and he finally woke up and went downstairs.

"Why were you under the bed?" Snow White asked.

"Because it was dark under there. Besides, I had the most wonderful dream," he said. "I was sleeping in a warm, cozy bed."

"But what about your dream, Princess?" Bashful asked quietly. "Aren't you scared?"

"Not a bit," Snow White replied. "Because I know it wasn't real. Some dreams are scary. Some are funny. Some are nice." She smiled. "But remember, one thing is the same about every dream. They're all just make-believe. They disappear as soon as you wake up!"

"I think it's time to make this breakfast disappear," grumbled Grumpy. And that's just what they did.